DEMON FLAMES

THE RESURRECTION CHRONICLES

M.J. HAAG

To every dessert and candy ever invented,
This is what happens when writing on a sugar high.

DEMON FLAMES

A world destroyed.
A species returned.

As hellhounds continue to roam and the zombie plague spreads, Drav leads Mya to the source of her troubles— Ernisi, an underground Atlantis and Drav's home. There Mya learns that the shadowy demons, who've helped devastate her world, are not what they seem.

Trapped in Ernisi, Mya tries to convince Drav to return her to the surface so she can continue her search for her family. However, he's determined to keep her where he knows she'll be safe. When Mya falls ill, Drav must choose between her and his people.

CHAPTER ONE

IT WAS ALL SO SURREAL. THE CONTINUAL RINGING IN MY EARS added to the despair of realizing the world around us was being bombed to hell. Drav's fingers bit into my side with each jarring stride as he sprinted to put more distance between us and the Army base. But, I barely noticed the ache.

Staring at the clouds of dust and smoke that rose into the air caused a numbness to spread through me. I'd survived so much in the last week. Zombies. Hellhounds. Now this.

In the distance, the second shockwave flattened debris with a devastating force that raced toward us. I ducked my head down and hung onto Drav with the same desperation he held me. His arms tightened, and he seemed to run faster. The force of the impact jostled him, but he didn't stumble this time.

I glanced up at him. Tears caused by the brightness of the sun streamed down his cheeks, dripping from his tense, stubborn jaw. That stubbornness had saved me. If he'd left like I'd wanted, I would have died.

I caught the sun's reflection off the large body of water to our right while I listened to the north side of Oklahoma City fall to its knees.

When the shockwaves no longer touched us, I peeked over his shoulder again. Trees blocked most of the view, but I still saw the smoke and dust-clouded horizon. My breath lodged painfully in my throat. My city, my home, was gone.

My family.

"Drav, stop. Put me down."

He immediately halted and placed me on my feet. Before I could look at the phone I still clutched, he clasped my face between his large hands. His squinted, worried gaze swept over me.

"Are you all right? Were you hurt?" he asked.

The panic in his voice warmed me. Even with everything I knew gone, I wasn't alone. I gripped his wrist with my free hand.

"I'm fine. Are you okay? That first aftershock hit us hard."

He nodded and, with a shaky exhale, set his forehead against mine. I appreciated the sentiment. My insides still felt like Jell-O. Leaning into his embrace, I released his wrist and placed my hand on his chest. Our breaths mingled while we stood in the relative safety of the trees, the distant continuing blasts emphasizing the fate we'd escaped.

"Drav, I need to call my family. I need to let them know I'm safe."

His hands slid from my cheeks to the back of my head.

"I need to know you're safe, too." The look in his eyes made my heart stutter for a moment, as did the way he gently trailed his fingers down the side of my neck. Emotions that I didn't have the time or luxury to examine raged inside of me. My breath caught at the feel of his fingers toying with the ends of my hair. Everything felt confusing when it came to him.

"I am safe," I managed to whisper.

He nodded and pulled back a bit.

Exhaling slowly, I tore my gaze from his and lifted my phone. I still had a signal. I half laughed and half cried as I fumbled to dial Ryan's number. Drav stood close, watching me, his thick fingers still playing with my hair.

Ryan picked up on the first ring.

"Mya!" His voice echoed like he had me on speaker phone. Hearing him cracked the hold I had on my frayed emotions. He really was alive.

"Mya, baby, are you okay?" Mom asked.

"I'm fine. We barely got out. I can't believe I'm talking to you." Silent tears choked my words. Drav's fingers immediately traced down my hair.

Mom began to cry, and Ryan's voice shook when he next spoke.

"Oh my God, Mya. I wanted to call you as soon as they turned the phones back on, but I was scared you had your ringer on and the infected would hear."

"It's okay. I'm okay. I'm safe. I promise," I said. "Where's Dad?"

"When we saw your text saying where you were, he went to try to stop the bombing," Ryan said.

I laughed through my tears. That sounded like Dad.

"You'll probably need to bail him out from somewhere. Where are you? I've been at least a day behind you. At the house. The cabin. The base."

"They're not telling us where we are."

"What? Why not?"

"Because they're afraid." His voice lowered. "There are some rumors that it's not just the hounds and the infected out there. I've heard something else showed up with the quakes. Something smart. Something the military's afraid of."

I met Drav's steady gaze.

"I don't understand what that has to do with them not telling you where you are."

"Whatever these things are, they can understand us. Communications went down to stop them from getting any potential information they might be able to use against us."

"Then why turn the phones back on?"

"They weren't going to. People here rioted when we heard the military was going to bomb the cities. Everyone is missing someone and hoping they're still alive."

"Cities?"

"Yeah." Yelling erupted in the background on Ryan's end and grew louder.

"Head north," Ryan said quickly. "There's more than one safe zone for survivors. Stay away from the cities."

The line went dead. Pulling the phone from my ear, I

checked the connection and immediately tried calling back. No one answered. A moment later, I lost my signal.

Without warning, I found myself once again holding my bag and cradled in Drav's arms. He took off running. The wind battered my face, but I didn't protectively duck into his chest again.

"Wait," I said, trying to breathe. "Where are you going?" I looked around at the blurring trees and the sky, trying to get my bearings. We needed to head north. Where in the heck was the sun?

"We must keep moving," he said without slowing.

The trees gave way to a few houses in the rural outskirts of the city as well as a hazy view of the sun before we ran under their cover once more.

"But we're going the wrong way. The sun needs to be on our right side."

"Listen," he said, maintaining his focus on running. "Do you not hear it?"

Ducking out of the wind, I concentrated on the sounds around us. The absence of bird song and animal chatter still creeped me out. That left the faintly discernible whoosh of our passage under the noise of the explosions going off— getting louder, actually—and the hum of the planes in the sky.

"What should I be hearing? The bombings or the planes?"

"Both. And they are in the direction you want to go. You have many cities, and they plan to destroy them all. You are not safe here. If I take you north, you will get hurt."

My stomach sank as I realized he was right. He couldn't take me north. Ryan had made humanity's fear of Drav's people clear. If Drav tried helping me reach a safe zone, he'd be the one hurt. I couldn't risk that. I had to reach my family on my own. Yet, the idea of leaving him upset me. This new world scared me less with him at my side. And, he certainly wouldn't like the idea of me going off on my own, either. However, the bombings would give me the cover I needed to use a different mode of travel.

"We need to find a road or a car," I said.

He veered out of the trees without question and found a quiet stretch of country road within minutes. He ran beside the worn blacktop, passing the occasional house. Nothing moved and there were no cars. I needed to figure out where we were.

"Stop," I said when I spotted a road sign.

Drav did as I asked, but he didn't set me down.

We were running alongside 60th Avenue. Perfect. Kind of. We weren't as far south as I'd thought.

From his arms, I eyed the quiet expanse of road. A few abandoned cars dotted the blacktopped length further south, near Highway 9. In the distance, heading north in our direction, I saw a few infected. They were sprinting toward the sounds of bombs and their eventual ends.

"This will work," I said. "If we find a car with keys, I can drive north. The infected won't bother me much. With all the bombing, they won't hear me unless they're really close. And in a car, the people bombing will know I'm not infected, and I'll be safe."

I looked up at Drav. The tears hadn't stopped streaming, and I wished Phutsy hadn't head-butted Drav and broken his sunglasses.

"It's not safe even with a car," he said.

"Look around, Drav. Nothing's safe anymore. Driving a car to where I need to be is the safest option."

He studied me for a long, quiet moment before moving toward the first car. The broken driver's side window gave a clear view of an infected woman strapped into the front seat. She didn't lurch forward or move anything but her head. Only her eyes tracked our approach, almost as if she was aware she couldn't reach us...that we needed to come to her.

"Skip this one. It's probably out of gas," I said, not wanting to get any closer.

Drav jogged to the next car. The driver's door hung open, the inside empty.

"Let me down so I can see if there are keys."

He set me on my feet and took the bag from my arms. I quickly found the keys in the ignition. The excitement at finding them died when the engine failed to turn over. Dead battery. However, after checking the visor, glovebox, and center console, I found another pair of sunglasses for Drav.

The dark lenses provided him a measure of relief and stopped the watering so we could continue our search.

We hit the jackpot with the fifth vehicle parked in the driveway of one of the homes on the road. The truck started on the first try and had a full tank. I looked up with a smile, expecting to see Drav standing by the driver's door. However, the space was empty. Across from me, the passenger door opened, and he got in.

"Uh…"

"Close your door, Mya."

"Drav, you can't come with me. Where I'm going—"

"You need me to get there safely. Now, close the door."

I frowned but did as he wanted. The sounds of the blasts were growing louder and the infected drawing closer. We didn't have time to argue out all the reasons he needed to let me head north by myself.

Shifting the truck into reverse, I backed out of the driveway and started south. I would take him as far as possible. When I found a place to turn west so I could circle around the city, I'd drop him off.

"Can you open the glove box? It's that compartment tucked into the dash right in front of you."

I swerved, trying to avoid one of the infected running at us but ended up hitting it anyway. Blood spattered the windshield, and I fumbled to figure out how to clean it off.

"What do you need from in here?" Drav asked, drawing my attention from the mess.

"A map, if there is one."

"There is," he said, pulling out an old map of Oklahoma as I crossed over a deserted highway nine.

"Good. Because the only roads I know heading north are the ones that cut through the city they're blowing up. See if you can find us a way around."

Paper crinkled beside me. I pressed the wipers again and

removed the rest of the blood in time to hit the next infected. I'd run out of washer fluid at this rate.

"I can't read this," Drav said.

"What do you mean? I thought you just needed to see a word to know it."

"No. Once I hear a word, I know it. Writing is different."

"Why?"

"I'm not sure. Maybe because we don't use writing."

"Really? Okay." With the road before us clear, I slowed down, not bothering to ease off onto the shoulder. There was no point without traffic.

"Let me see the map," I said, once I stopped.

"Wouldn't it be easier if I drove and you told me where to turn?"

"You can drive?"

"I think so. The pedal on the right makes the vehicle go. The pedal on the left makes it stop. The wheel gives it direction. The handle beside the wheel cleans the glass."

"There's a bit more to it than that. Just hand me the map."

Drav passed me the map. As I studied the map, he began to run his finger lightly up the length of my arm. I shivered and peeked up at him. All of his focus remained on gently stroking me. I swallowed then slowly leaned away and focused on the map.

After a few moments, I figured out the route I would take to drive around the city so I could head back north.

Something thumped into my door, making me jump and

squeak. A boy around my age, stared at me with cloudy eyes. He swayed side to side on his feet, his mouth gaping open and close. Behind him, I saw another infected sprinting our way, attracted to the sound of our engine instead of the distant blasts.

Sliding the shifter back into drive, I took off, continuing south.

"Is it just me or are they getting creepier?"

"You've always found them creepy," Drav said, watching the road in front of us.

"And you haven't?"

"No. Not creepy. Unpleasant and numerous."

I couldn't argue with that. The two infected fell behind, and I paid attention to the road ahead. Because of the river, I ended up driving all the way down to Lexington and through Purcell before heading north-west on I-35, more than an hour after the bombing had begun.

The attempt to stop and drop off Drav failed completely. He refused to get out. I couldn't say I experienced any disappointment over his unrelenting refusal to leave me, yet I did worry about what would happen to him when we reached our destination. I didn't want him to get hurt.

As we drove, a solid, light grey filled the sky to the east. Not just above Oklahoma City, but off in the direction of Tulsa, too. The bombers were destroying everything. I understood why. Getting to the military base had been hard. The infected far outnumbered the survivors. Bombing had been an easy way to kill them and the hounds. But what about the shadow men like Drav? I glanced at him. They were different, overly clueless about girls, and prone to acts of violence. Yet, they weren't all bad. Especially not Drav. I hoped his people wouldn't die because of the explosions.

Despite the destructive activity to our right, we continued north at a reasonably steady pace. Some people must have tried evacuating on the highway earlier, because the further north I drove, the more cars we saw crowding the road. A heavier degree of dust had settled on them, as well.

A jaw-popping yawn made my eyes water as I navigated through the abandoned vehicles. I leaned forward, trying to see through my yawns and the silt covering the windshield.

"You're tired," Drav said. "Stop and rest or let me drive."

I was exhausted, and Ryan's crappy "head north" directions likely meant we had a lot of driving in our future. It would be easier if I taught Drav how to use the truck now.

"Fine," I said, slowing. I slid the gear shift into park. "The letter P stands for park, R for reverse, and D for drive." I pointed to each one as I spoke then moved to open my door.

"No," he said, grabbing my arm.

I glanced out my window, expecting an infected. Drav's hold vanished, and his fingers gently traced over the sleeve of my hoodie. I looked at him.

"I didn't mean to hurt you," he said softly.

"You didn't."

He brushed his fingers along my cheek and smiled slightly.

"I'll get out. You slide over. It's safer if you stay in here."

He opened his door and missed my blush. Trying to control the summersaults in my stomach, I once again

11

realized how thankful I was that Drav had refused to leave me.

A second later, he climbed into the driver's seat and glanced at me, as if making sure I had truly remained safe for those few moments he'd left. Apparently satisfied with what he saw, he buckled his seatbelt and focused on the truck. I watched him move the shifter into drive while keeping his foot on the brake.

"Good," I said, impressed. "Now ease off the brake and gently give it some gas with the right pedal." The truck lurched forward then smoothed out into a steady acceleration.

"Go slow until you get a feel for steering and stopping," I said, feeling a little nervous.

He wove through the vehicles and even stopped to move one out of the way. My mouth popped open when I saw him lift the back end of the sedan. He swung it off the road with ease then got back in and took off without a hiccup.

"Rest, Mya. I'm comfortable driving."

"You're not tired?" I asked. "I don't want to crash because you fall asleep at the wheel."

"No. I'm not tired yet. I'll wake you when it's your turn to drive."

I willingly closed my eyes. The steady sound of the tires on the road and Drav's presence lulled me into a restful sleep.

CHAPTER TWO

THE TRUCK SLOWED, ROUSING ME SLIGHTLY. THE SOUND OF the door opening and closing finished the job, and I groggily opened my eyes. The bright light of the sun blinded me. It took a few blinks to focus and understand why we'd stopped.

Two abandoned cars sat crossways in the road, blocking our way. I frowned at the odd sight. No way they'd been left like that accidentally. The thought had barely formed before Drav lifted the back of one and took a step toward the shoulder to clear a path for us.

In the space of a heartbeat, four infected emerged from the new gap between the cars and ran at Drav. My mouth fell open in shock. Drav dropped the car and ripped off the head of the first one. The spray of blood bathed the remaining three as Drav tossed the head away. The infected didn't seem to notice the loss of their companion as they circled Drav.

One lunged at Drav from behind, its teeth snapping at Drav's sizable biceps. Drav turned swiftly, barely avoiding being bitten. However, the other two used the distraction to charge forward. My heart jumped, and I shouted a warning.

With a burst of speed, Drav pivoted and moved behind the snapping infected. While he ripped off its head with a quick jerk, one of the remaining two gave up on him and sprinted toward the truck. Toward me.

I slammed the locks down. It didn't matter that the infected couldn't open my door. Going from a nice, peaceful nap to a zombie attack had freaked me out, as had the idea that the cars had been positioned in the road on purpose. But, by what?

Breathing hard, I looked up and came face to face with an infected. The woman's stringy brown hair hung over her pallid face, but not enough to stop her milky white eyes from tracking my movement inside the truck as I eased away from the window. Drool spilled from her gaping mouth.

One moment her dead eyes stared at me, and the next, Drav stood in her place, his green eyes full of life and anger. He chucked her severed head over his shoulder and stalked around the front of the truck. It took a moment for me to see he'd already moved both cars.

I unlocked the door, and he slid into the driver's seat, his leg pressing against me. Even with the way clear, he didn't immediately start driving. He gripped the steering wheel tightly and stared straight ahead.

"Drav?" Hesitantly, I reached over and touched his arm. The hard muscle twitched under my fingers.

"Are you okay?"

"Do you see how dangerous it is for you?" he asked, not looking at me.

"Yes, I do." I patted his arm soothingly. "But you don't need to worry. I'll be safe with my family. Where they are is safe."

He turned and met my gaze. The intensity in his eyes, behind his sunglasses, made my stomach flutter.

"I will protect you, Mya."

I wasn't sure if he said it for my sake or his own. Giving his arm a gentle squeeze, I scooted back to my side of the bench seat and buckled up.

Drav put the truck into drive and focused on maneuvering us through the scattered vehicles. After the past week of being in the dark, it felt odd being awake while the sun still sat high in the sky. As more miles passed quietly, I relaxed and closed my eyes, lulled by the motion of the truck.

Blood spattered dreams, showcasing my family with milky white eyes, plagued me until the truck slowed.

My door clicked open, jolting me, and the cool air brushed against my skin. I blinked my eyes, trying to focus.

"I have you, Mya." Drav's gravelly voice brushed against my ear.

I turned my head toward the sound and found him leaning over me to unhook my seatbelt. Once freed, he scooped me against his chest. I looped my arms around his neck, snuggling close with a sigh. Something brushed my temple. It took a moment for the sensation to have meaning. A kiss. The gesture warmed me.

"I can walk," I said, making no effort to pull away.

"This is safer." He started moving, and the steady motion comforted me more than it should have. Traveling in Drav's arms sure did feel safer. I relaxed and started to drift sleepily, but my stomach growled loudly and brought a measure of reality back. I was hungry because we'd been running since sunrise.

I lifted my head and glanced around. The sun hung lazily on the horizon.

"Why did we stop?"

"The truck stopped making noise."

I bit back a groan of frustration.

"We probably ran out of gas."

I studied our surroundings. We were stuck in the middle of nowhere, and there wasn't another vehicle in sight. A vehicle had been ideal while near the cities, but as those four infected on the road had proven, we were hitting quieter areas. And with the sun rapidly dropping, the noise of a vehicle would not only attract the infected but also the hounds.

"It's probably for the best. Are you tired yet? Should we find somewhere to rest?"

"No. You need to eat."

Instead of arguing that he'd gone days with little sleep, I tugged the bag from his shoulder and cradled it on my stomach so he could run without making any noise. He picked up his speed, and I turned my face into his chest. The wind whipped past, whistling in my ears for several minutes before he slowed.

Glancing up, I saw an old farmhouse. He placed me on

the screened-in wraparound porch and told me to stay while he checked inside. The world remained eerily quiet while I waited. However, the sound of all those explosions continued to haunt me. Were the planes still out there destroying cities? I wrapped my arms around myself and hoped the bombings had stopped. It would be one less problem I needed to worry about. I still had to figure out how to find one of the safe areas without Drav getting hurt in the process.

As if my thoughts had summoned him, he returned. In the fading light, his gaze swept over me. I could see the tender concern in his eyes.

"Come," he said softly. He held out his hand, and I threaded my fingers through his.

He led me into the little house's foyer where stairs led up to the second floor. Passing by those, I followed him through the house to the kitchen in the back. I spotted a switch and turned on the lights.

A small breakfast table was tucked next to the big picture window. He told me to sit while he searched the cabinets. I glanced out the window at the lowering sun, and my stomach tightened both with hunger and nerves.

My family waited for me out there somewhere. How would we ever find them? We had so much working against us.

The thump of Drav setting a couple of cans of food on the table interrupted my thoughts.

As I looked down at the fruit, tuna, and Spam, I finally noticed the infected blood speckling Drav's hands. Hands that

MJ. HAAG & BECCA VINCENZA

I'd just held. I quickly looked at my own. Although the blood didn't appear to affect Drav, it still posed a threat to me.

"Wait, we need to wash up."

I stood and went to the sink, scrubbing my hands with soap. After I finished, I turned and found Drav just behind me. I squeaked and looked up at him.

Infected blood splattered his forehead and cheeks, several little dots close to his eyes and mouth.

"Wow. You really got them good. Or, I should say, they got you good. Just a sec."

I searched the drawers near the sink for a towel. Finding one, I wet it with a bit of soap then faced Drav. He hadn't moved. Mid-way to handing him the towel, I changed my mind. Without a mirror, he'd never get it all.

"Let's move to the table after you wash your hands."

He quickly scrubbed his hands free of infected blood. His shirt remained spattered. I considered digging in my bag for a clean one then changed my mind on that, too. If he didn't plan to spend the night here, he'd probably just get dirty again, anyway.

As soon as he sat at the table, I stepped between his open legs and began to wipe away a small spatter of blood closest to his eyes.

He exhaled slowly. A tug on my sweater caused me to look down. Drav's fingers curled around the hem and held tight. I knew it wasn't fear. He just liked hanging on to me. I might have smiled a little when something started to swirl in my belly at that thought.

Moving to the other side, I continued to clean away the

blood spatter. When I finished, I took a new cloth and wet it to rinse away any soap residue. His fingers once again toyed with the bottom of my shirt.

I hated knowing that he would be in even more danger now because of me. Any human who spotted us together would think Drav had taken me and was dangerous, just like Charles had. Drav would not only need to work at keeping me safe from hellhounds and infected, but he would need to keep himself safe from humans, as well. We had so much stacked against us.

When I finished, I pressed my forehead to his. He closed his eyes at the contact.

"Thank you," I said.

"For what?"

"For everything."

I went to place a kiss on his cheek, but he turned his head at the same time so my lips landed on the corner of his mouth instead. His hands suddenly gripped my sides. Not painfully, but possessively. I pulled back quickly. His gaze held mine for a moment while my face heated. Then, he slowly released me.

Escaping, I returned the towel to the sink before washing my hands once more. I took my time, letting the warmth in my face cool and the butterflies in my stomach calm. When I felt more in control, I turned off the water.

Drav watched me closely as I walked to the table and sat down again. I didn't know what to say or do, and his intense look and lack of response made me even more on edge.

A rumble from my empty stomach gave us both

something else on which to focus. Drav pushed a can of food toward me.

"Eat, Mya."

I wrinkled my nose at the Spam and pushed it away, choosing mandarin oranges instead. All the cans had pull tabs, and I immediately opened mine. Drav watched me fish out an orange wedge and pop it into my mouth before he grabbed the tin of Spam that I'd scooted away.

He popped a hunk of gelatinous meat into his mouth and chewed. I watched his reaction, waiting to see what he thought. Based on his expression, he liked it. When he caught me looking, he offered me some. I declined, and he ate the rest while I finished the oranges and then some tuna.

Drav pushed another can toward me.

"I'm full," I said. More than that, I couldn't waste any more time on food or whatever had just happened between us. I had to find my family.

Before I'd been chasing after hope, but hearing from Ryan and Mom had changed hope to reality. Even though I knew they were protected by a fence and men with guns, I also knew all the dangers that waited out there. I doubted there was anywhere truly safe anymore.

"Are you okay to keep going?" I asked. "We could probably find another car to use until the sun goes down."

"I'm okay, Mya. But, don't you want to sleep a little more?"

"No. We need to get moving."

The longer we stayed, the more my stomach knotted. With the bombs and the weird infected behavior on the road,

I worried that we wouldn't be able to travel at night as swiftly as we had been. It felt safer to keep moving while we had a bit of daylight remaining.

We left the farmhouse after I stuffed some cans of food into my bag, which Drav shouldered. Once outside, he didn't ask if I wanted to be carried. Instead, he picked me up and began running before I could even protest. Not that I would have. He could get us there faster—where ever "there" was—if I wasn't slowing us down on foot.

With a sinking feeling, I realized he'd left the map in the truck.

"Drav, we have to go back and get a map."

"We don't need it. I will keep running in the trees alongside the road."

I reluctantly agreed. Although, I would have felt better with the map, I didn't care for the idea of backtracking and wasting precious time. We could check cars along the way.

The sun dropped closer to the horizon as Drav ran. A pretty sunset peeked through the trees, and the soft, warm reds and oranges slowly began to darken. Although breathtaking, something about it felt wrong. Ominous. Unable to figure out what, I tucked my face into Drav's chest to avoid the wind until he suddenly slowed.

"What's wrong?" I asked, looking up at him.

His attention snapped to the right, toward the remnants of twilight. In the distance, a howl echoed, followed by another. A shiver chased through my body.

Hellhounds.

"Hold on tight," Drav said.

He took off faster than before. I squeaked and put my head into the crook of his neck to protect my face. The air whipped past us, lashing at me with icy fingers.

A howl sounded closer, and Drav quickly changed directions. Snapping branches and a sharp snarl jerked me from my protective cocoon. I peeked over Drav's shoulder and caught a flash of glowing red eyes. The dark shape wove through the trees, slowly closing the distance between us. Behind it, another set of red eyes flashed.

He tightened his hold on me. Fear swam in my stomach. Would we be able to outrun them? I had no idea who was faster. Drav or a hound? He and I hadn't seen any since the night we'd met. Sure, Drav had dealt with that pair, but I would prefer he not stop to fight these two.

The trees blurred with Drav's speed, but the hounds were still too close. Drav took a sharp turn and dodged around some trees.

Ahead, something flickered through the barren treetops. A second then a third appeared. Houses. Maybe if we—

In the dim light before us, more shadows moved. My hope that we could make it to a house, or somewhere safer, died. They had us surrounded.

Drav didn't slow, though. He ran straight toward the oncoming numbers, shadows that moved...familiarly. I squinted into the wind, trying to see better, and finally grasped that the shapes were much too large to be hounds. Demons. Shadow men. Drav's kind.

The first one blurred past us. A snarl, followed by a grunt, sounded in our wake. Three more men sprinted by us. I glanced back and watched them work together to face the oncoming hounds. The first beast yipped in pain when one of the men tore its jaw away. Trees blocked my view from seeing anything further. Still, I listened for signs of anything coming after us, until Drav slowed.

I faced forward again to see the trees giving way to the end of a house-lined road. Street lights illuminated the two shadow men waiting for us.

"Drav," one said.

"Kerr. This is Mya. She is a female."

Kerr's mouth dropped open, and the man next to him grunted in disbelief. I realized, with that one word, we'd just bypassed the whole no-penis talk.

"Hi," I said, politely.

"Asking to see her breasts or pussy makes her uncomfortable—"

"Geez, Drav!"

"And she does not like to be smelled or touched without permission."

Kerr's mouth snapped shut, and he stared at me. I glared up at Drav.

"I can't believe you just said that."

"You want them to smell you?" Drav asked, frowning down at me.

"Of course not."

"I don't understand."

"Just...never mind. Is it safe to put me down? Are your friends killing the hellhounds?"

The man with Kerr said something in their language,

stealing Drav's attention. Drav answered in kind.

"I don't like when you do that," I said. "They understand what you say when you say it in English. But I can't understand you when you speak your language."

Drav glanced down at me but kept talking, throwing in a few words like Ghua, Phusty, no penis, smell, and dead to clue me into his conversation. I waited for outrage, accusations, or anger. But, there was none. The two men listened impassively.

I peeked back at the trees and saw the blood-spattered men who'd run to help us, standing behind Drav. They listened intently to Drav's explanation of what had happened with Phusty. Each one of them watched me, but none had the aggression that Phusty had immediately shown.

When Drav stopped speaking, they remained quiet. I glanced up at Drav after a moment. I didn't have much experience with his kind. Sure, Drav was great and Ghua had been okay. However, the whole fighting thing with Phusty, because he wanted to see my bits, still had me slightly unsure.

"Does this mean they are going to be okay with me?"

Drav's gaze held mine, and he nodded.

"No fighting?" I asked.

"No fighting."

I glanced at the men again, knowing they understood everything we'd just said. Their expressions remained mildly curious, without any hint of aggression, and they continued to stare.

"Then, can you put me down? My legs are starting to hurt."

He grunted and gently set me on my feet. I kept an eye on the others while I casually stretched my legs.

"Come. We'll walk for a while," Drav said. He seemed to sense my hesitation around our new companions because he set his hand on my lower back and led me forward. The others fell in step around us.

Drav's abbreviated and slightly crude introduction seemed to have done the trick. No one made any move to sniff, touch, or get close to me. They stared, though. A lot. Since they'd never seen a girl before, I could understand the gawking. Maybe being around so many of Drav's kind should have made me nervous, but I felt more relief than anything else. They'd just proven how useful traveling in numbers could be.

We walked down the center of the quiet street. A few cars sat in driveways, making me wonder if it wouldn't be wiser to travel by vehicle. This area seemed quiet, but how far were we from the next big city? I looked at the cars again, thinking about at least looking for a map before I realized it wouldn't do me any good. I had no idea where we even were. At the corner, I glanced at the street sign, which only showed a numbered avenue. No help there.

Three infected came running at our group from behind the corner house. Drav lifted me into his arms as two of the group dashed to meet the infected before they got closer. In seconds, three heads went flying and the headless bodies fell to the pavement.

"You are safe, Mya," Drav said.

I looked up at him, slightly amused by how quickly he'd

snatched me up and reassured me. He didn't look amused. Worry creased his brow as he set his forehead to mine. I reached up and smoothed a hand over the back of his head.

"I know I am," I said softly. "Thank you. Can I keep walking for a little longer, though?"

Reluctantly, he let me down.

A pretty, birdhouse-style mailbox caught my eye on the side of the far street, and a brilliant idea struck.

"Can we go look at that?" I asked. After the hellhounds and the infected, I wasn't foolish enough to move more than three feet from Drav's side.

He walked with me as I veered toward the mailbox. I opened it and wasn't surprised to see an empty cavity. The hellhounds had attacked Oklahoma late at night. It was unlikely that the mail had been delivered after the attack. But there had to be at least one person in this neighborhood who'd forgotten to take in their mail.

I kept checking mailboxes while we progressed down the street, until I found one with a letter. I grinned and pulled it out. My grin slowly faded. I didn't know the town, but I knew the state. Texas. The ominous foreboding I'd felt when staring at the sunset clicked into place. The sunset had been to our right, not our left.

Drav had admitted he couldn't read the map, yet I'd closed my eyes as soon as he'd offered to drive so I could rest. What had I really thought would happen? I'd been dictating our direction since the moment we'd met.

"Drav," I said, looking up at him. "We somehow got turned around. We've been heading south instead of north."

CHAPTER THREE

D<small>RAV GLANCED AT</small> K<small>ERR AND THE REST OF THE MEN BEFORE</small> meeting my gaze.

"Yes, I know," he said.

Was this some kind of man thing where he couldn't admit he'd gotten us lost? Or had Kerr already told him where we were? I needed a crash course in their language.

"What do you mean, you know?"

"It is not safe to talk here," he said. A noise further down the street confirmed his words.

"Come." He opened his arms to me.

I frowned but quickly went to him. Held safely against his chest, I only freaked out a little when a group of six infected appeared between two houses. They ran toward us, a united mass of movement...except for one. Its right arm flapped uselessly, barely attached by a bit of gore. The mangled mess of meat had me cringing more than their numbers.

The rest of the shadow men moved forward with almost

military precision to meet the attack while Drav hung back, cradling me in his arms. With quick efficiency, Drav's friends proved his head ripping tendencies a common trait among his kind. Finished dealing with the infected, they once again surrounded us and kept pace with Drav as he sprinted through one neighborhood after another.

I watched the passing scenery over Drav's shoulder and began to notice trees leaning heavily to the side. Leaning turned to uprooted trees laying in yards, broken windows, and one partially collapsed house. My stomach dipped with worry. Earthquake damage. How close to Irving were we?

"I don't think we want to go any further south," I whispered against Drav's neck. "Are we almost there?"

"Almost," he said.

Any signs of houses, yards, streetlights or even trees, abruptly stopped. Moonlight cast long shadows on piles of wood, shingles, and twisted siding where houses once stood. Pot holes and chunks of blacktop replaced the smooth surface of the road.

My throat tightened as the destruction grew to the point where I could no longer identify what had been house or road or yard in the weak moonlight. Hints of smoke and burnt rubber or plastic tainted the air, and I buried my face in Drav's shirt. I didn't want to see more anyway. Bombings had wiped everything out and left ruin in its wake. If they did this to every city, what would be left of our world?

I thought of my parents and Ryan and wished the phones still worked. Did the military understand what the bombings were leaving behind? Ryan probably did. But what good was one teen against terrified adults with heavy artillery. I realized it could have been worse. At least whatever they were using to destroy the cities wasn't nuclear. I frowned. I hoped it wasn't nuclear...

"We really need to get out of here," I said against Drav. "It might be dangerous to breathe this air."

"We're getting closer," he said.

I lifted my head for a quick peek and immediately ducked back down out of the wind.

"Closer to what? There's nothing left but rubble," I said. I started to wonder how the shadow men could possibly run through it all. As though he was reading my thoughts, Drav jumped over something, and my stomach dipped like it did when I drove over a hill too fast.

"Somewhere safe where we can talk," he answered.

He ran tirelessly, weaving, clambering, and jumping over debris to get to wherever his friends were leading us. Suddenly, he stopped.

"Mya, I can't carry you like this. I need you to hold onto my back."

Drav set me down and tossed my bag to Kerr. I studied the dark area, puzzled.

In the dim light of the moon, our six companions surrounded us, watching me closely. Beyond them, several other shadow men stood encircling a large area of shadowed ground, facing outward as if guarding the space from the darkness beyond. If they were guards, they weren't very good at it because they kept casting occasional glances our way. To be fair, though, we were the only living things as far as I could see. Beyond us, there was nothing but dirt and stone.

"Your arms got tired?" I asked, looking at Drav.

"No, Mya. I could carry you forever."

The tender way he said the words made my cheeks heat.

"I don't understand, then," I said, glancing around once more. That's when I noticed one of the guards looking down and to his left. I followed his gaze and realized the dark area I'd assumed to be shadowed ground was actually a pit. A very, very large pit about the size of an Olympic swimming pool.

I tore my gaze from the darkness and looked up at Drav.

"What's going on?"

"It's not safe up here, Mya. You could die," he said softly.

Disbelief and understanding slammed into me.

"You brought me here on purpose? You turned us around on purpose? I trusted you!" I slammed my hands against his chest, trying to push and hurt him at the same time. The blow didn't move him.

A frown creased his brow, and he caught my wrists and tugged me toward him. I stomped on his foot, then hit him again when he released me.

"Asshole! Fucking asshole!" Tears of frustration and anger welled in my eyes. "My family is waiting for me. They are alive, Drav. Finding them was the whole point of everything we've done since the moment I met you."

"I know, Mya. I'm sorry. It's too dangerous to try to reach them. Your people are willing to kill you to destroy the infected."

"They didn't know I was there," I yelled.

His impassive expression remained unchanged with my words. Seeing my anger had no effect, I stopped pushing him and moved closer to set my shaking hands on his chest. I licked my lips, took a calming breath, and looked up at him.

"Drav, please. You helped me get home and to the cabin and back to the base. You've kept me safe. I know we can reach the safe zone. Please." I didn't care that I was begging. My family thought I was on my way. I knew they were worrying as much as I worried about them.

His fingers brushed the tears from my cheeks, and my hope surged.

"No, Mya. We're not going back. We're going to my home now."

"Fuck that." I pushed away from him, wiped my eyes, and glared. His betrayal hurt. A lot. And I refused to literally disappear from the face of the planet just because he couldn't get over his worry that something would happen to me up here. The idea of walking away from him terrified me. But, was he really leaving me with any other option?

"I'm not going with you."

He exhaled heavily and reached out to gently smooth back my hair.

"I am not leaving you, Mya."

I swallowed hard in relief.

"Good. Let's go." I turned away from his touch and made it about three steps before he stood in front of me. He stooped low in a familiar move and tossed me over his shoulder. Anger and disbelief coursed through me. He wouldn't...

He turned and moved back toward the pit, answering my doubt. Furious, I twisted and kicked and tried to escape his hold. The other shadow men watched, their gazes curious, but made no move to help either of us.

"Put me down," I yelled, not caring if I attracted an infected's attention.

Fisting my hands, I hit his back. His large palm came down with a crack on my ass cheek. The pain robbed me of breath and stilled my struggles.

"Give me the rope," Drav said in very clear English.

"I swear to God," I choked out, "if you tie me up, I'm going to kill you."

His hand smoothed over my sore butt.

"I won't tie you, Mya. Hold on."

With that, he turned, and I found myself staring down into a black abyss. My stomach did a nosedive to my toes. I grabbed Drav's shirt just before he hooked an arm around my legs and stepped back into nothing.

As we dropped into the darkness, my scream echoed around us, followed by a gruff laugh from above. It took a moment to understand we weren't falling. Drav's muscles rolled beneath my hands, and his hold on my legs tightened and relaxed rhythmically. He was climbing down. Very hesitantly, I lifted my head.

"Don't move, Mya. We'll fall."

The warning was enough for me to plaster myself against him. Drav continued to climb steadily downwards, his shoulder rotating under my stomach, creating a bruising ache. How far were we descending?

"I'm never going to forgive you for this," I said into the darkness.

His movements hesitated for the briefest of moments before resuming.

"I understand."

"Since you've never dealt with a girl before, I really doubt you do."

I blinked several times and tilted my head to look down again. My eyes seemed to be playing tricks on me because I thought I saw something.

My stomach jolted when we dropped suddenly. Drav's shoulder jammed into my stomach as his feet hit solid ground. I grunted and tried to free myself. He held tight.

"Put me down."

"I'll carry you."

"Put me down, or I swear I'm going to start biting." My voice shook with anger and unshed tears.

"You will not be able to climb up the rope. The others are coming down."

I slapped his back, annoyed that he had easily guessed my intentions. It didn't matter that rope climbing wasn't my strong suit or that Drav would have stopped me before I'd made it more than three feet or that I was almost blind. At this point, I just wanted to put some space between Drav and myself.

"Your shoulder is hurting me. Put me down."

Instead of doing as I asked, he flipped me over and cradled me in his arms.

"You will not be able to see. It'll be safer if I carry you."

He walked forward down what felt like a steep slope. While the blood rushed back out of my head, I looked around, straining to see, and realized it hadn't been my imagination that I could see again.

A subtle glow from the crystal on Drav's wrist illuminated the area. I looked over his shoulder and saw several more glows behind us and a brighter one still several feet above. One for each of our six companions.

In the weak, slightly blue-tinted light, I could see the dark rock walls of the tunnel.

"It's light enough for me to see, Drav. Put me down now."

His shoulders lifted with a heavy sigh. But, instead of fighting me, he put me on my feet then steadied me by placing a hand on my arm. I shrugged off his hold and stepped away.

"Kerr, walk ahead of Mya."

Kerr slipped past us, his bracelet lighting enough of the dark that I saw the different shades of color in the walls. I also saw my pack on Kerr's shoulder.

"Can I have my bag back, Kerr?"

"It would be better if he carried it. The path is steep," Drav said.

"Kerr?" I said, ignoring Drav.

"Mya, it—"

"I'm not talking to you," I snapped.

Kerr said something, but of course, I didn't understand a word.

"I hope that was a yes," I said.

Neither man spoke.

"My flashlight is in the bag."

"It's not safe to use it yet," Drav said quietly.

Semi-blind, I angrily followed Kerr. My foot slipped and loose stones tumbled down the rocky slope. And, they kept tumbling, the sound growing quieter but never really ending. Just fading away.

"I'm going to die down here," I said to myself, jerking away from the hand Drav had used to steady me.

It took effort to maintain my footing on the slow-going hike downward. Between that and the increasing temperature, sweat plastered my hair to the back of my neck in no time. My head began to ache and my clothes felt like I had sweated out all the moisture in my body.

Just when it started to feel like a never-ending march, the slope bottomed out. Two steps onto the even surface, a tingling sensation rushed over my skin and my ears popped painfully. I blinked back my tears and kept shuffling forward, wondering at the sudden drop in temperature. On the third blink, I froze and looked around in stunned awe.

The area before us stretched further than I could see. And I *could* see.

Ethereal blues and greens lit different type of rock formations rising up from the cavern floor. I realized the unique designs, with their crude edges and unsymmetrical patterns, could only have been made by nature.

Weird strings dangled from the ceiling further into the cavern, lighting the way and giving this area its breathtaking, subtle light. Underneath the strings to our right, a still pool of water reflected the beautiful glow.

It all seemed so surreal. Why did that surprise me? I had been taken into this pit in the Earth on the shoulder of a demon man, while hellhounds, infected, and humans destroyed the world up top. Unreal no longer seemed to have the same meaning it used to.

One of those demons walked past me and quickly scooped some water into his hand from the still pond, jolting me from my thoughts. He moved to the side while he drank. I'd forgotten about the others in my surprise.

I twisted to look behind me. Rock, shaped like a series of frozen waterfalls, bordered a gaping blackness where the light didn't reach. The rest of the shadow men were magically emerging from the hole's gloom.

"What the hell?" I half-whispered.

Drav stood near me, watching but saying nothing. The final man gradually appeared. A leg then torso and head emerged as if he'd stepped through a curtain of invisibility. It let me know that something insubstantial had kept me from seeing Drav's world until I stood in it.

I took a step toward the dark, wanting a closer look, but Drav blocked me.

"You're not leaving, Mya."

"You're a tool, Drav," I said, turning away.

Kerr stood behind us with my bag. He handed it over with a nod then moved to where the others crowded around a small cave in the waterfall rock formation. They sifted through the group of weapons piled there. Knives, long walking stick things, and bows.

Drav watched them for a moment then turned toward me.

"Stay. I will be right back."

He turned away from me before I could flip him off. Pissed, I looked at the magical darkness that led the way home.

CHAPTER FOUR

WHERE THE HELL WOULD I GO? I THOUGHT ANGRILY.

Sure, that black abyss promised a way back to the top. But, it also led to a place where I wouldn't be able to see and to a rope I wouldn't be able to climb. Even if I could somehow manage to reach the surface, I would be facing infected-central alone and without the vehicle I'd counted on to get me to a safe zone. In what world would I have any hope of making it out of the city and further north without help? Definitely not the world I currently lived in. I was at Drav's mercy, and it pissed me off.

Bending down, I dug through my bag until I found my water bottle. Nothing swished inside when I shook it, and I berated myself for forgetting to refill it at the farmhouse.

Glancing at the pool, I wondered how safe the water would be to drink. Sure, the shadow man had done it, but he came from here. However, since I knew finding a nearby faucet wasn't going to happen, I didn't see that I had much choice but to do the same.

Kneeling beside the pool, I dipped my hand into the cool water and brought it to the back of my neck to bathe away the sweat. The second handful, I lifted to my mouth and bravely took a drink. It tasted a little like lake water, but it wasn't too bad. I let it settle in my stomach for a moment, debating the chance of it making me sick. The world was falling apart, and I was in my own underground hell. Why not throw in some dysentery? I scooped both hands into the water to take a bigger sip, partially quenching my thirst.

Not knowing when I'd get another chance for a refill, I dipped my bottle into the water. Ripples raced out over the previously calm dark surface, making the reflection of the green glowing lights from above dance prettily.

Mesmerized, I leaned over the edge of the pool, wondering how deep it descended. Something moved in its depths. Before I could see what, the water erupted.

Time slowed as a fish with knitting needle like teeth rose toward my face. In frozen fear, I stared at its bulbous eyes.

A sharp tug pulled me off my knees just before the thing reached my face. As I fell backwards, Drav stepped in front of me, his wide shoulders partially blocking my view. He drew back his arm, spear in hand, and skewered the fish through its gaping mouth before I landed hard on my butt.

My pulse pounded in my ears while I stared at the writhing creature.

Drav tossed it and the spear to the cave floor then turned to me. The thing gave a final flop, then stilled. My shaky breaths echoed in the sudden silence, and I looked up at Drav.

His wild, rage-filled eyes swept over me before he squatted next to me and cupped the back of my head. I readily leaned toward him, pressing my forehead to his, needing the feel of safety that only he could provide.

"Those waters are not safe, Mya." He threaded his fingers through my hair and rubbed his forehead lightly against mine.

I exhaled shakily.

"Yeah, I see that."

"You must be careful." The chiding way he said it rekindled my anger. I wouldn't have needed to be careful if he hadn't dragged me down here.

I pulled away from him and got back to my feet. The others watched us like we were some daytime soap opera.

Kerr made a comment in their language. Ignoring them, I capped the half-full bottle I still clutched in my hand.

Drav moved away from me, picked up my bag, and lifted the strap over his head to settle it on his shoulder.

"You can walk for a bit, but we need to move fast, and I will need to carry you."

I didn't bother saying anything. He wouldn't give me a choice anyway.

Kerr led the group out, and Drav nudged me so that I would follow right after Kerr. The other men spread out around us. They carried spears in their hands now, gathered from their supply pocket back in the cavern. The three before us had bows strapped to their backs and a quiver of arrows attached to their waists. Drav carried a spear in his hands. The sudden need for weapons now made me nervous since it just hit me that Drav hadn't used any up top. And, the way he had used the spear on the fish with such precision showed he was no novice.

A few of the men drifted closer as we walked through the massive rock formations. As we threaded our way between the structures, I couldn't help but notice the difference in shapes. Some looked like pillars reaching up to the weird lights on the cavern ceiling. Others looked like clusters of misshaped, upside down ice cream cones. Bits of glowing moss clung to the tips, making me think of distant snowy mountains.

While we walked, I tried to come up with some reason that might persuade Drav to bring me back to the surface. The need to find my family motivated me but held no meaning for him. All he seemed to care about was keeping me safe.

"I don't understand," I said angrily. "You thought you could keep me safe before. Why change your mind now?"

"Your people are bombing the cities."

"So what? We could have driven around the stupid cities!"

"No, Mya. You have many, many cities. No more talking. It is too dangerous."

"If it's so dangerous, why'd you bring me down here?" I whispered harshly.

Kerr said something softly and Drav grunted but didn't answer either of us.

I fumed and marched on.

At times the pillars and other formations crowded so closely, it felt like we were in a large tunnel, rather than a cavern. The confining space in some places meant we walked close together, making it hard to ignore the not so subtle sounds of sniffing around me.

The further we walked, the better I began to see. Not that it helped.

The shadow men moved expertly through the tunnels. Drav reached out constantly, steadying me each time I tripped over rocky areas. I barely stopped myself from smacking his help away each time. Yes, I was angry, but was it smart to piss Drav off when I wanted him to take me back to my world? Probably not.

The tunnel opened wider ahead of us, and a brighter glow came from that space. I glanced at the men, but neither Drav nor any of the others were squinting.

Suddenly, Kerr rushed forward, two others following after him. They reached the opening and waved us forward.

"Yeah, yeah. I'm hurrying," I grumbled, looking down to watch my feet once more. If I tripped again and Drav grabbed me, I'd deck him. Screw the consequences.

A warmer breeze brushed my hair back, and I looked up just as we reached the opening. For the second time since dropping into hell, I forgot to be angry and stood in awe.

The crowded cones and pillars in the first cavern had nothing on this new one. Its massive roof rose three times as high, making it at least six stories overhead. Imbedded in the ceiling, jagged glowing crystals illuminated the area in a soft blue light. Four giant columns rose up near the far end of the space, the only large rock formations. Fernlike vegetation, interspersed with white, stunted skeletal trees, filled the rest of the cavern. From those skeletal trees, small brown globes hung from thin branches, like an eerily beautiful orchard.

"What is this place?"

The sound of my voice startled something in the blue-green fronds a few yards in. Kerr whipped his bow up and let an arrow fly. The bolt shot forward and disappeared into the growth. The rustling didn't stop but zipped away from us toward the trees.

Kerr gave me a disgruntled look and stalked forward to retrieve his empty arrow. I didn't understand why he was upset. The thing—whatever it had been—had run away from us, not toward us.

"I don't know the word for this place," Drav said from beside me, nudging me forward. "It's an old place where we grew epella."

I'd forgotten I'd asked something, and it took a moment for the last word he said to sound familiar.

"Apples? This really is an orchard?" I studied the brownish spheres doubtfully. A sheen of blue light reflected off the almost opalescent dark skin.

"Yes. An orchard. A very old one that still produces a good harvest."

Drav picked a globe and offered it to me. I glanced at the fruit then him. Did he think a kind gesture would remove the sting of his betrayal? I walked passed him, trying to ignore the squeeze of my heart.

Skirting around the trees, we moved through the ferns. Their feathery tips brushed my fingers. I would have reached out to feel them, but the way the men remained alert made me nervous. Kerr had his bow ready with an arrow notched.

"What was that thing running through the ferns, anyway?"

"Food," Drav said.

No wonder Kerr had looked annoyed. I'd scared away dinner.

"So there are a lot of animals down here? Are they all like the hellhounds?"

"Yes, there are many animals but not like the hellhounds. The hellhounds are not food. The other animals are."

"Oh." That was good. No...not really. It was a little concerning that he didn't consider the other animals like the hellhounds after that fish had tried to eat my face. I glanced at his killer fish spear.

"If you all had weapons, why did you leave them down here when you went up top?"

"We didn't go up top to hunt."

Kerr said something, sounding impatient. Whatever Drav said back held a warning tone that shut him up.

"What did Kerr say?" I asked.

"He said he thought you weren't talking to me."

"Kerr can bite me."

Drav growled low at my words and stepped defensively in front of me. I rolled my eyes and looked around him to Kerr, who had stopped walking and was rattling off a string of unintelligible words at Drav.

"Kerr will not fight you," Drav said angrily. "Not without a life crystal."

"Fight? I said bite me. You know...like kiss my ass."

Drav's head swung around to me, his expression one of shock. I groaned in frustration.

"You are way too literal. It's a saying." I looked at Kerr. "Bite me isn't a challenge to actually bite me. It means shut up and mind your own damn business."

Kerr grunted and turned away to resume walking.

Drav straightened, still studying me. I decided to address Kerr's not talking comment to set Drav straight.

"Just so we're clear, I haven't forgiven you, and I don't trust you anymore. While I know there's a very good chance you'll lie to me again, no one else knows enough English to answer my questions. So, yeah, I'll talk to you, but I'm still mad enough to hate you."

I sidestepped, planning to go around him, but he shadowed my move, blocking me. I glared up at him.

"I will take your anger gladly," he said, his gaze holding mine as he reached up to caress my face. I jerked my head away from his touch.

"We'll see."

I stomped my way through the ferns, following after Kerr and trying to ignore the rest of the men. Something small ran right in front of me. I squealed and backpedaled at the flash of fur, red eyes, and horns.

Drav was right there, putting a comforting hand on my shoulder. In no mood for comfort, I swatted him away and soldiered on, mumbling the entire time about grey skinned assholes who thought they knew everything, face-eating fish, and jackalopes.

"Fucking jackalopes aren't supposed to be real. Obviously, this place didn't get that damn memo."

Something bumped into the backs of my legs. I flung my arms out as I fell backwards...into Drav's arms.

"You make too much noise," he said, softly. "Not all the hellhounds found the way out."

"I wouldn't be making any noise down here at all if we'd stayed up top like I'd wanted. We can still turn around." Although I'd said it quietly, I'd still managed to convey a satisfying amount of anger. I wasn't going to just give in to the abduction.

He exhaled heavily and leaned forward. I turned my head away, rejecting his version of a hug, and crossed my arms, refusing to make this any more pleasant for him than it was for me. He had the nerve to nudge my neck with his nose and inhale deeply. A shiver chased through me, and his hold tightened before he straightened and started walking. My reaction gave me an uncomfortable idea that I immediately rejected. I would not stoop to using my body to negotiate my way back home. Nope. Not happening.

"I'll carry you until we reach the source," Drav said, softly.

"What's the source?" I asked before I could stop myself.

"The place we recharge our life crystals."

"Life crystals?"

"Shh," he said a moment before the light began to fade.

I looked around and saw we'd stepped behind the giant

columns. There were no trees in their shadows, only a sparse growth of stunted ferns that dwindled with each step that Drav took toward the dark void ahead.

A cool draft of air brushed my face. I uncrossed my arms to hold onto Drav more securely. He shifted me higher, and I looked over his shoulder at the light we were leaving behind. Too late, I remembered the flashlight in my bag. The threat of hellhounds was enough for me to swallow any request for it. If they weren't already in the dark, I didn't want to call them.

Drav moved forward steadily, a soft glow coming from his wrist as well as the wrists of the other men around us. Being so close together created a small bubble of visibility, allowing me to see. The cavern we were now entering had craggy rock formations, but they were broken up by occasional pools of still, dark water. I leaned into Drav, grateful he carried me. I did not want to fall into one of those pools while stumbling around in the dark.

Thankfully, the dark was short lived, and the creepy cavern merged into one that had numerous, small green-tinted crystals poking from the ceiling. Once again, I noticed a change in temperature when we crossed from dark to semi-light and wondered what it meant.

The group picked up its pace until Drav was sprinting. Each cavern we passed through appeared slightly different than the last, and I always felt some subtle change in temperature or moisture. The caves didn't stretch in a linear grouping but in a webbed network of interconnecting spaces.

Finally, Kerr stopped in a cavern with a small waterfall.

The water churned near the fall but smoothed out into a sizable pool further away. The dim blue light from the crystals above reflected prettily on the surface, which I was not going near.

"We'll rest here," Drav said, setting me on my feet.

"By the water?"

"No, over here."

He attempted to thread his fingers through mine, but I pulled away.

"I can follow without being tugged or nudged."

He frowned but led the way to an area of ferns and rocks. I followed hesitantly, remembering the jackalope. When nothing jumped out and the ferns remained quiet, I took the last few steps to where he stood on a mossy patch of level ground.

He stomped on a bunch of surrounding ferns, tamping them down to create a Drav-sized area in which he lowered himself and stretched out.

"You mean we're sleeping here?" I said, eyeing the ferns once more.

"Yes, Mya. We both need sleep."

I'd managed a nap in the truck—how long ago had that been?—but he hadn't slept since the first night in our cabin.

With an expectant look, he motioned for me to join him.

"Not happening."

"Mya, it's safer sleeping with me."

"Pft. Snuggling up next to you was fine when we were on the surface and you were actually helping me."

He frowned at me, but I ignored him and checked out

what everyone else was doing. A few men stood in nearby positions, creating a loose outward-looking circle around us. The rest had done the same thing Drav had and were already laying down in their own little nests. I moved a yard away from Drav, stomped down my own spot, and settled in.

The blue crystals scattered above almost looked like stars. Big ones. Instead of closing my eyes to sleep, I stared at them and wondered about my family. Were they worrying? Had Dad convinced someone to help him look for me by now? Were they still safe? I sighed and tried to think of nothing... especially not creepy horned rabbits hiding in the tall grass.

Eventually, I slept.

CHAPTER FIVE

MALE LAUGHTER AND DRAV'S VOICE NEAR MY HEAD WOKE ME.
I lay on my side, comfortably warm with Drav curled around
me. His arm draped over my waist and a hand rested on the
skin of my stomach under my shirt. For a sleepy moment, all
was right in my world. I was warm and safe because of the
man holding me close. Then, reality came crashing back.
He'd taken me from the surface. From my family. Against my
will. And now, the jerk had cozied up to me while I slept.

I elbowed him hard and rolled away. He grunted and
frowned up at me while I glared at him.

"There was a reason I laid down here. I didn't want to be
by you."

Another smattering of laughter came from the others,
and I gave the sources a dead stare.

"Laugh again, and I'm feeding you to the face-eating
fishes."

My threat didn't wipe the grins from the men's faces, but

it did stop the laughter.

I stood up and cringed when I realized what I'd need to do next. In a large cave filled with ferns, a waterfall, and an unsafe-for-humans swimming pool, there wasn't one place a girl could relieve herself that was private and safe.

Drav got up with a sigh.

"Are you hungry?"

"No." I really was.

"Are you thirsty?"

"No." I could drink a little.

He gave me an indecipherable look then moved toward the water's edge where he relieved himself. One of the other men got up from his spot and did the same. There was no way in hell I would dangle my ass over the water after what happened yesterday. I'd hold it.

I sat down in my fern nest and tried not to think about how hungry or thirsty I was. Thinking about either made all my physical discomforts harder to ignore.

The two men finished their business. Then, to my relief, they went to the waterfall to get a drink. I noticed another man sitting by a nearly flat boulder. On his way back from the water, Drav picked up something from the surface of that rock and popped it into his mouth. He caught me watching and said something in his language to one of the other men. The man grunted, took something from the stone and came toward me, holding out his hand.

"Mya, food," he said, squatting beside me.

I looked at the shiny clear bit of jelly looking stuff in his palm.

"What is it?" I asked.

"Food."

This language barrier thing sucked.

"Am I going to die or get sick eating it?"

"No."

"Is it gross? It looks gross."

"No."

I sighed and picked up the clear glob that felt much firmer in texture than it appeared. I sniffed it. It didn't smell like much. A little fishy. I popped it in my mouth and almost gagged. With everyone watching me, I choked it down with a shudder.

"Was that raw fish?"

"Yes," he said.

"Yeah, I'm not a fan. Thanks, though."

He stood and moved back to the others who were eating more clear bits from the rock. That explained why Drav liked the canned tuna fish. The thought had me jolting to my feet.

"Where's my bag?"

"Mya," Kerr called, holding it up from where he had laid it in the ferns.

I waded through the fronds to collect my bag then sat down not far from him. He leaned on one elbow and watched me dig through my supplies until I produced a can of peaches. I had my finger on the pull tab, ready to open it, when reality stopped me. There were four cans of food in my bag. Four. The piece of fish, while disgusting, had eased some of my hunger for now. If I had a drink, I'd be fine. It would be smarter to save the canned food for when I really needed it. After all, I had no idea how long Drav would make me stay down here.

Half-growling at the reminder of how much control Drav had over my fate, I stuffed the can back into my bag. When I stood and placed the strap over my shoulder, my need to go to the bathroom could no longer be ignored.

I glanced at the seven sets of eyes trained on me.

"I have to pee. Since I don't have a dangler like the rest of you, I'm not peeing in the water. I'm going to go over there," I said, pointing to a taller group of ferns, "and all of you are going to stare at the waterfall until I'm done. Agreed?"

"No," Drav said, standing up.

I saw red, picked up the nearest loose rock, and threw it at him with an angry yell. The jagged stone clipped the side of his head, making him jerk.

"It's not enough you took me from my family?" I seethed. "Now you're going to take my dignity?"

Without taking his gaze from mine, he stalked toward me. I held my ground, glaring and wishing for another rock.

When he reached me, blood dripped freely from his head.

"I'll watch the opening behind you," he said, his words calm and quiet.

Not waiting for any reply, he moved toward the tunnel entrance beyond the tall growth of ferns and stood there with his back to the rest of us. Kerr rose, then gave me a censuring look before joining the other shadow men.

A sharp pain stabbed at me. Though I tried to swallow it, I couldn't. Even down here, with me telling him how much I hate him, Drav still protected me.

Guilt and shame curled inside me. Drav hadn't taken my dignity, but I'd lost it all the same. Trudging to the ferns, I set my bag to the side then dropped my pants. I cried and peed. Both, fairly quietly.

I hated that I'd thrown the rock at Drav when he'd only been trying to, yet again, keep me safe. What I'd done was wrong. Just like making me come down here against my will was wrong of him. I couldn't take back my actions, but he could take back his. He, however, refused. With that thought, some of my anger returned.

Finished, I pulled up my pants with a cringe. I hoped wherever we were going had a shower. Wiping my eyes, I took a calming breath before picking up my bag.

"I'm done," I announced.

The others, who talked quietly near the falls, left their positions and gathered up their weapons. Kerr picked up a bow and spear then nodded toward me. I glanced back at Drav. Blood dripped from his earlobe to his shoulder, and he wore a wary look on his face.

"I need to carry you again," he said.

I felt guilty I'd hurt him but not sorry. Too much anger still boiled inside for me to feel remorse. I hated where we were and what it had done to us. I wanted to hug him and bring the closeness back. I wanted to trust him again. But I couldn't. He hadn't just taken me from my family, he'd robbed me of what I'd thought we'd had together.

"I shouldn't have thrown the rock," I said. It was as close to an apology as he would get from me.

"We should stop the bleeding or you'll end up fainting

and falling over on me." I knelt beside my bag. The first aid kit wasn't elaborate, but it had gauze and some tape. I grabbed what remained of my water and stood.

"You might want to take your shirt off. I'll need to clean the blood away to see what I'm doing." I shook the bottle for emphasis. Not that it was needed. He had his shirt off in a heartbeat.

He sat where he had been standing and looked up at me. The others waited near the tunnel where Drav had stood guard. Kerr gave me an impatient look. I rolled my eyes at him and went to Drav's side.

Using the last of my water, I began to rinse away the blood.

"I know you are still angry with me," he said softly. "Do you want to throw another rock?"

"I already said I shouldn't have done that."

"Yes." He set a hand on the back of my calf. "But you did what you felt you must do at the time. Just like I did what I felt I must to keep you safe."

His hand slid down the back of my calf. The gentle stroke made my pulse leap. It also made my temper flare.

"Keep it up and I'm kneeing you in the face," I said softly, not pausing my work.

He removed his hand from my leg, but his gaze remained locked on my face. Ignoring him, I set the water aside and took a bit of gauze to press to the wound. I'd gotten him good, and it would take a while for it to stop bleeding.

"I thought beauty meant the way the crystals lit the water in the caverns or the way the inuchu flower blooms in the dark," he said, drawing my attention. "But I was wrong. Beauty is seeing the soft look of concentration on your face as you touch me. It is seeing your peaceful face and parted lips as you sleep beside me. It is the look in your eyes when you search for me as soon as you wake."

Heat rose to my cheeks that had nothing to do with anger. With those simple, earnest words, he'd reminded me just how much I meant to him and it tore at me.

He truly didn't see what he'd done as something wrong. He'd only been protecting the one thing that mattered to him most. Me. Unable to stop myself, I set my hand on his cheek before quickly stepping away.

Bandaged and cleaned up, Drav put his shirt back on and lifted me in his arms before I had a chance to join the others. He looked down at me, his gaze intense. Then he leaned closer. My heart hammered hard in my chest as he glanced at my lips.

Kerr said something, halting Drav's advance. When I looked at the man, I found him half-smirking. Heat burned my cheeks. I couldn't believe I'd almost let Drav kiss me after a few pretty words. Swallowing hard, I focused on reigning in my emotions.

"What did he say?" I asked.

Before Drav could answer, Kerr's expression changed. He spoke a smattering of loud words. From somewhere behind us, an answer filtered its way back.

Drav turned and I saw Ghua, jogging toward us through the ferns.

"Drav," he said. "Mya."

Behind him, his companions carried Phutsy's body. I'd forgotten about them and their need to return home.

"Ghua, I'm glad you made it," Drav said.

The men carrying Phusty's body followed the edge of the pool, circling toward the shadows on the far side of the water.

"Any signs of them?" Drav asked.

Ghua answered in his language while glancing at me.

"Tell Molev we're coming. We must go to the source first."

Ghua nodded, said something with my name mixed in, then turned and jogged toward the party disappearing into the darkness.

"What did he just say? And let me just add, I'm glad we're not going that way." I was tired of dark caves.

Drav moved toward Kerr while he spoke.

"He is going to our city to tell Molev, our strongest fighter, what happened between Phutsy and me. He is also going to tell Molev about you."

Great. Good ole Ghua was running ahead to tell an all-male city that the first female ever was on her way. Fear reignited my anger.

"You shouldn't have brought me down here. It's not too late to turn around and take me back."

Drav picked up his pace and said nothing.

With no sun, I couldn't tell how much time we spent traveling through the subterranean maze. We took several breaks, mostly so I could stretch my legs. Drav always stayed close while the other men watched me with open curiosity from a distance. Both actions frustrated me.

During one of the breaks, Kerr got lucky with his arrow and shot a jackalope. Hungry, and no stranger to wild game, my mouth watered at the thought of cooked rabbit. Kerr, however, didn't light a fire once he skinned the critter. He butchered it and started handing out raw chunks of meat that the men immediately began to eat. I quickly shook my head when he offered me my share.

"Mya, you need food," Drav said from behind me.

"Not that." I wasn't nearly starved enough to consider munching on some raw jackalope.

ONE OF THE oddest things about Drav's world was the lack of normal sounds. No wind rustled the leaves. Nothing chirped or sang. I found the silence eerie, but that changed the first time something did make a sound.

As we approached the next large pillar, something rustled the grass then became still. A noise rose that started out like an infant's cry then morphed into the creaking sound of a rusted door, slowly opening. Goosebumps broke out on my arms. Creepy and mournful didn't begin to describe the noise.

The rest of the group made a rapid halt while Kerr jogged forward with his bow. A thump almost immediately followed the thwang of his arrow. Drav and the others quickly moved forward.

Beyond the column, I could see Kerr going to the deer

he'd killed. The thing looked completely normal. Brownish fur. Antlers. Brown eyes.

Having had venison before, I couldn't say I was sad to see Kerr hit his target.

"If you cook that, I'll definitely eat," I said.

All the men turned to look at me with serious expressions.

"No, Mya. That is not food," Drav said, turning and moving away from the men.

I arched my neck to look closer at the deer as the rest began working together to skin it. The creature had hooves, no claws or anything. Its teeth weren't jagged or threatening. I wondered why they didn't eat it.

"You said everything down here but the hellhounds was food," I reminded him. "If it isn't food, why did you kill it?"

"For the skin. We use it to make clothes."

"And you waste the meat? Seriously, I'll eat some of it. Give me a fire and a stick, and I'll hot dog that thing."

Drav stopped walking and considered me for several long moments.

"I can't. Not even for you." He set me on my feet. "Stay close. When they are finished, we'll move again."

It frustrated me that the one thing that looked edible was off the menu. Not that I would argue. They lived down here, and I didn't. If Drav said something wasn't food, I wasn't going to put it in my watering mouth.

Sighing, I walked circles in the soft grass until I noticed the light fading. I blinked up at the crystals, wondering if something was wrong with my eyes. Kerr called out, holding up the skin.

As he rolled it up, a baying howl echoed in the air around us. Further away, the grass rustled as jackalopes sprinted in the other direction, running from the threat of the hound.

Drav had me up in his arms before I could panic.

"It smells the blood," he said.

He continued in the direction we'd been headed. At least, I thought it was the same direction. The rest of the group hurriedly fell into place around us.

More baying joined the first, and the sounds kept getting closer.

I looped my arm around Drav's shoulder, and the wound on his head caught my gaze. Red dotted the white. I glanced behind us. Four of the six men ran in our wake. Beyond them, fifteen red eyes blazed in the sea of darkness. No... sixteen. I was pretty sure one of those fuckers had just winked because that pack of hellhounds had skipped the deer for better prey.

My act of pissiness was going to get us killed.

"WE'RE ALMOST THERE," Drav said.

I looked forward and saw a bright light in the distance.

"They won't enter the source."

"Neither will we if you can't run faster," I said.

He did. I alternated between watching the distance between us and the light filled opening versus us and the salivating hellhounds.

Halfway to the source, Kerr and his friend, who were

running in front of us, stopped. Drav raced past them without hesitation. The others stopped as well. The six men faced the oncoming pack. Eight to six wasn't bad odds, I hoped. After all, Drav had taken on two hellhounds, and we'd survived.

The two groups clashed with yells and growls. The hounds jumped and circled the men but didn't pursue us. I watched as Kerr, using Drav's spear, stabbed one in the side. The beast didn't fall.

Distance and the lack of light blurred the details of the battle, until the men and hounds disappeared from view. I looked toward the spot of light that I thought was the source and watched it grow larger until we stepped into a different cavern. The bright light after so much darkness made my eyes hurt.

Drav lowered me to my feet and hugged me hard, almost suffocating me. I pushed away, needing to breathe and still angry.

"Enough, Drav," I said, pulling my head back to glare at him. "What is your deal?"

He released me and spun me around so I faced the source of light. This cavern was smaller, about the size of three football fields. Ferns, grass, trees, and other strange vegetation grew in a dense tangle around an odd formation of crystals in the center of the space.

The massive cluster of crystals extended down from the ceiling and up from the floor, creating an hour-glass shape. A white-blue crystal connecting the two, pulsated with life and power. My stomach churned uneasily, looking at it.

"Go, Mya. Touch the source."

"Uhh…why? What's going to happen?"

He stepped in front of me and earnestly met my gaze.

"Nothing bad. The source keeps us alive. Safe. I need you to be safe, too."

I narrowed my eyes at him.

"I don't trust you."

He frowned slightly, stepped aside, and pointed.

"Follow the path."

A thin trail led through the growth to the crystal in the middle. Fear shivered over my skin at the sight of the glowing source.

"No."

He tossed me over his shoulder, turned around, and started for the crystal.

"Drav! Dammit!" I hit his back. "You can't do this every time I disagree with you," I yelled.

He didn't stop until he stood right before the glowing mass.

"Touch it," he demanded.

"I don't want to. I'll probably explode."

"You won't explode. It feels pleasant when you touch it."

"Yeah, right." I went to cross my arms, but he grabbed my hand. I guessed, whether I wanted to or not, I was going to touch it.

He gripped my hand and stretched it forward. A sickening feeling rolled through me a moment before the pad of my finger pressed against the pulsing light.

My breath left me, and everything around me changed.

CHAPTER SIX

A GROUP OF WOMEN AND MEN, ALL MOVING WITH SILENT GRACE, walks between the colossal trunks of towering trees. The simple muted colors of their clothing blends well with the forest. If not for the pale perfection of their faces, they barely appear visible. Intricate braids adorn their long, silken hair and allow a view of elegantly pointed ears.

"Here," one of the women says, stopping and looking up at the nearest tree. "It weakens."

"We will give it strength," another says.

Each individual steps forward and sets their hands on the ancient bark. A soft glow lights their palms and spreads into the bark. One of the women faints after only a few seconds. The rest remove their hands and sit heavily upon the earth.

"The forest is dying," a man says. "The more it weakens, so too do we. It is time to send scouts to search for a new home."

The woman on the ground rouses enough to speak.

"Yes, it is time."

. . .

I INHALED...

TEN MEN RUN TOGETHER through the trees. Nothing stirs at their quiet passage, despite their impressive speed. Ahead, a light appears a moment before the trees give way to a sunlit body of water. Ten large boats wait upon the shoreline, along with other fey.

A woman, regal and beautiful beyond compare, stands apart from the rest, watching as farewells are made and each boat fills with ten men.

"Be blessed on your journey." She steps forward and touches the first boat. The vessel moves away from her as if she's pushed it out to sea. She does the same for the remaining boats then stands on the shore until they fade from sight.

I EXHALED...

THE BOAT SCRAPES against the rocky shore. The first man nimbly jumps from the vessel and touches the soil as the rest gather up the supplies.

"There is strength here, but muted," the man says to the others.

A fey from the boat throws out a travel bag and looks at the shoreline.

"The trees are so small," he says.

"New, perhaps," the one on shore says.

"Perhaps," he agrees.

The group of ten set out from the boat, exploring the trees together. A deer startles not long after they enter the forest.

"A good sign," one says as they move on.

The trees and wildlife are abundant the further they move inland. They stop often to touch the earth and the vegetation, sensing a strength in this new place, a strength different from their home. After several hours, they spot something that makes them stop.

A primitive woman in furs and leathers gathers berries from a nearby bush. Her skin, the color of wet sand, is darker than theirs.

"She is pretty," one of the men says softly. "And, another good sign."

The rest agree and quietly move away to continue their exploration of the new land.

On the second day, something subtly changes. The strength they sense when they touch the earth now touches them in return. With growing excitement, they trace the source to a cave entrance.

"This is unusual," one says. "The power feels so similar to the heart tree." He thinks of the largest and oldest tree in his ancestral home —a single tree that provides shelter to a third of his people. Meanwhile, the rest of the group debates exploring the caves.

"We are not hill dwellers to live underground," one says.

"We are not. However, it is wise to understand the strengths of this new land in every form."

They agree that exploration is needed, not just of the cave, but the land, too. The group splits. Five to explore the caves and five to continue exploring the land. An agreement is made to meet at the cave entrance in three days.

After those exploring the land leave, the others step into the darkness, taking turns to use their power to light the way, until the first one shudders and disappears from view. He reappears a moment later.

"There is a barrier here. Magic like none I've felt before. Come see for yourself what it hides."

One by one, the men step forward and disappear from the darkness and appear in a cave lit from above by beautiful glowing crystals. Wonder fills them at the sight of vegetation and a few animals.

"This is no hill dweller home," one says softly. He thinks of the short men and women who search the earth for metals and stones. His people trade with the hill dwellers often for the metals they find, and he knows their rustic dirt-filled dwellings.

"No," another agrees. "Let us explore further."

They wander the cave system, feeling the barrier occasionally when passing from one cavern to the next.

"I think this place is larger than it seems."

"And not pleasant everywhere," another comments when they step into the first of several caverns, all dark lifeless places with still pools of water.

Finally, in a cavern filled with crystal light and apple trees, they decide to rest.

"It is odd to sense it is night, but not to see the stars or moon."

"That is why we will never live in these caves. We are people of the earth and sky. There is no sky here."

One man lays down and looks up. "No sky or moon, but the crystals glow like stars."

"They do seem to flicker," another says, staring up. After a moment, he glances at a nearby pillar. Near the top, a cluster of crystals peeks from the stone ceiling.

He starts for the column.

"What are you doing?" one asks, setting aside his hard-biscuit dinner.

"I want a closer look." The man agilely climbs the pillar and clings to the surface at the top as he reaches out to touch the crystal.

A room fills his mind. Bright and bursting with light, it beckons. He releases the crystal and joins the rest.

"There is a cavern here filled with these crystals. I believe the crystals are the source of the power we're feeling. Not just here, but throughout the land. To connect to the power of the land...to survive... we will need to connect with the crystals."

"How do you know?"

"When I touched the crystal, it showed me."

"We will look for the cavern after we rest," another says, picking up his own hard-biscuit.

"We should have hunted before entering the cave."

"We can hunt here. Perhaps one of those horned hares."

Two of the group split off to hunt while the other three rest. The hunters trace their way back to a vast cavern filled with unusual trees. There they startle a doe, which they quickly bring down with an arrow. They thank the doe for giving her life then clean her and carry her body back to the others, along with branches from a nearby tree.

Working together, they start a fire and begin butchering the small deer.

"Look up," one says. "The crystals no longer glow. They stopped as soon as we lit the fire."

"We'll cook quickly and put it out again," one says, seeming troubled.

The fire crackles, and the smell of roasted meat fills the space. The men hungrily take their portions and put out the fire. There is a brief darkness before the crystals come to life again.

Near the group, the deer, once a carcass, suddenly jumps to its feet, whole and healthy and very much alive. After a moment, it takes off running. The stunned men stare. One sets down his skewer of meat.

"*This place is unnatural.*"

"*Unusual, but beautiful and with endless bounty, it would seem.*"

"*We should leave this place,*" one of the men says. *Another nods in agreement. They both decline to eat the meat, choosing the dry bread.*

The others exchange looks before taking up their skewers and biting into their portions.

I INHALED...

THE GROUP of five steps out of the cave into the blinding light of day. The other group, who had explored the lands, is already there waiting.

"*Brothers!*"

The men embrace each other.

"*The lands are plentiful of game and harvest. But full of humans,*" *one of those who had remained above ground says.*

"*Humans?*"

"*Like the one we saw gathering. They hunt and gather but do not farm or harvest. They live together in caves. Tell us what you found.*"

"*The caves are the source of the power we sense in this land. And full of hidden secrets. Come, we will show you.*"

Together, the large group explores, reaching further into the cavern's depths. Each cave is different. Some are filled with greenery and crystals and trees while others are dark and filled with pools of water or empty of everything but stone. Some caverns are so vast the men need to rest before continuing. Through it all, the newcomers are in awe of the things they see, and find themselves brushing their fingers over the odd fruits and greenery.

One man, with familiar-feeling bright blue-green eyes, steps up to a small tree, plentiful with fruit. He plucks a small brown globe from the thin branch and brings it to his nose. The sweet smell fills his nose and makes his mouth water. But he does not eat the fruit. He puts it in his sack and joins the others who are nearby. One of his brethren brings a finger to his lips for silence.

Ahead, three of the fey stalk a deer. The buck lifts its mighty head, ears flickering between its massive antlers. The men move with agility and swiftly take the buck down.

The hunters reverently thank the buck for its sacrifice as the others join them.

"We will need much wood to cook and dry the meat for such a large kill."

"No. That is part of the magic here. Watch."

The men work quickly, taking only the choicest pieces of meat while leaving the body otherwise untouched. The meat is set aside, and the men step away from the buck.

"We do not waste like this," one of the newcomers says.

"Watch," another says, motioning the others back.

High above, the crystals pulse with power. Energy surges from the ceiling down the walls and into the ground. The men feel the recoil of it as they watch the buck twitch. The skin knits back together, muscling filling in the void beneath where it has been removed.

It doesn't take long for the buck to recover. The others stand in awe as it jumps to its feet and bolts away. The two, who had declined the meat, share a look of apprehension. The others are in awe.

"It's alive."

"And whole."

"This place provides endless meat but no sun," one of the two objectors says.

All the men look up to the forever night sky.

"We have much to learn about this place," the one who'd collected the apple says quietly. "Were you able to connect with the plants?"

"We did not yet try."

"And we did not hunt outside to know if all deer are reborn. Let us separate again. Four of us will return outside the caves to hunt. The rest should continue to learn more about these caverns. We will meet at the entrance in two days."

Two from the original party in the caves choose to return to hunt outside. The six who remain inside travel slowly and continue to learn what they can of the magic of the place. However, what they learn is limited. When they touch the trees and plants, they feel the power coursing through the stems and trunks, but they cannot direct it to encourage growth and health.

Touching the crystals themselves always shows the men the same vision of a light-filled room. The men set out to find the main source of the crystals and unravel the mysteries of the underground world.

A small group of three walks into a cavern illuminated brightly with white-blue light. Crystals descend downward from the ceiling and upward from the floor to form a pillar in the center of the room. In the middle of the pillar, a solid, huge crystal connects the top and bottom.

Magic pulses from the crystal source so strongly, the men feel it in the air. The fey who'd plucked the fruit steps forward to the cluster of crystals and touches the center stone. Power surges through his veins. He places his other hand on the crystal and gently presses his forehead against the cool, calming surface.

A flash of light blinds the room for a moment. When it fades, the fey steps back from the crystal. Cradled between his hands is a small crystal glowing softly. A symbol is etched onto its surface.

"What happened when you touched it?" another asks.

"It welcomed me to its home and gave me this gift. I can do more than feel the energy now," he says.

He opens his pack and removes a seed. He bends down and places his hand with the crystal on the stone floor over the seed. The soft glow brightens in pulsing waves for a moment. When the man removes his hand, a small mound of soil cradles a tiny sprout.

"With the crystal, I have a connection to the source."

The next man moves forward and presses his forehead to the source crystal. The same light flashes, and he too steps away with a crystal, making room for the next to receive his.

The six each spend time working with the energy in the room until each has coaxed a plant to grow for them.

"We should go back to the entrance and tell the others," the first says.

They agree and return to the beginning with their crystals.

The men emerge from the caverns, and their eyes water at the harsh light of the midafternoon sun. It takes a moment for them to see the others standing around two fallen deer a distance from the opening.

One of the hunters spots them and waves them over.

"We hunted this one in the caves and brought it out. This one is from the woods. Neither has revived."

"Perhaps we need to wait longer out here where the power isn't as strong," one of the new arrivals says.

"Or perhaps we try to use the crystals," another says.

"Crystals?"

The six with the crystals explain what happened in the source cave, and one of the skeptical fey speaks up.

"You should have left the unnatural magic down there."

"The crystals are of the earth as are we. Thus, the magic is not unnatural, just different. Do not fear something because it is new and unknown. We were sent out with a purpose. To find our people a new home. This land is full of life and energy. We must learn what we can then let our people decide."

No one objects after that, and the six step forward with their crystals. They wait for the familiar rush of power to revive the deer, but nothing comes. They try for hours, which turn into a day.

The deer do not come back to life.

I EXHALED and an involuntary shudder ran through me...

TEN FAMILIAR MEN stand on a shoreline and face a group of older fey, just disembarking from a ship. Thousands of ships dot the waters on the horizon.

"Welcome," one of the men says.

"Greetings. What have you found here?"

"These lands are different than our homeland, new and not yet grown. Yet, there is so much power in this thriving place. Can you feel it? Even here on the sands?"

The older ones nod.

"There are caves further inland, the source of this land's power. The animals there revive. We will never have to worry about starvation. Plant life grows in abundance."

"You say the animals come back to life?" one of the Elders questions with a hint of eagerness.

"Yes."

"Tell us more of this new land."

While the ships moor, each of the ten imparts to the elders some of what they have seen or learned. The two objectors share their concerns about nurturing a magic that would so cruelly bring back to life an animal only to see it slain and eaten again and again. The elders listen with care to everything then dismiss the explorers so they may discuss what they've learned.

The rumors of the wonders of the caverns spread throughout the fey. More men come to the original explorers to listen to them speak about the land and what it has to offer. Many inspect the crystals.

Almost a month's time passes as the elders consider the new land. During that time, the elders visit the caves with the original explorers and learn more of its magic, creatures, and terrain. The main body of settlers stays near the shore and makes temporary homes in the trees. Not in the branches, but on the forest floor. They begin to farm, planting the seeds they brought with them from their dying homeland.

Under the elders' watchful presence, the explorers use their crystals to encourage growth, but their connection with the power above ground is weak. The elders grant the original ten explorers permission to use seeds in the caverns. The men work tirelessly. What grows is different from what they knew in the homeland but not bad.

The elders make note of their bountiful results and require the explorers with crystals to surrender their connection with the source while they continue to deliberate. Everyone waits, wondering if this new land will become their home.

When a meeting is called, the people gather among the trees and listen. The ten explorers have places near the front of the crowd.

Four of the elders stand before the gathering.

"We have made our decision. We will remain in this land, but we will not live in the caves. The power goes against the laws of nature. The laws we live by," the eldest woman on the council says.

One of the explorers steps forward.

"The power in our home is dying. With its death, we lose our connection with the earth and plants. We will become just like the human cave dwellers and will have no power to nurture nature. We have proven we can bond with the power in the caverns and influence the nature there. The power is neither good nor bad, only the intent of the user. With this new source, our people and way of life will not die out."

"No. We will live above ground and connect with the power of the earth here."

"The power here is not of the earth, like our old home, but of the crystal. Truly, you must all feel the difference in power. There is no malice in it," the one who had been gifted the first crystal says. "To survive, we will need to connect with the crystals."

"Enough. The decision has been made."

"You have decided on behalf of the people. I ask to be allowed to decide for myself. I wish to live in the caverns."

"Then you are not of the people. The cavern lands are forbidden."

Denial rises from some of the men in the crowd. During their time waiting, they had heard of the energy that the crystals offered.

The first to receive his crystal turns from the elders and makes his way through the crowd. Others follow, until just over three hundred men split from the main tribe and begin their journey to their new home.

I EXHALED...

.   .   .

"WE CANNOT ALLOW them to return to our lands," an elder says to another.

"What do you propose we do?"

"Seal them inside, taking their memories of their lives with us. To help them understand the fault in their thinking, we will curse the deer within the caverns. Each time their flesh is consumed, they will return a shadow of their former selves."

The others on the council agree.

"We will need many of our people and the power of the six crystals for this banishment."

The elders chip away at the small cluster of crystals and take pieces of the broken crystal to give to the people.

Over one hundred of the oldest fey squat to the Earth, pressing their hands against the soil. They sing to the trees and Earth and bend the power of the land to their will. The Earth rumbles and shakes. The singing grows louder, weaving a web of power over the minds of the men now in the caverns.

The Earth closes over the entrance to the cavern, blocking out any way into the underground realm. With the unnatural magic locked in along with those who chose to use the magic they should not bear.

The Elders remain in place as they finish the curse upon the men who have gone against their laws.

"MYA..."

I inhaled painfully...

THE LIGHT FEY move from the place they had temporarily called home to escape the memory of brothers, cousins, and friends, who no longer live with them but remain trapped under the soil and a constant sour reminder of the sacrifices made. The elders weaken as the power of their homeland fades.

The fey begin to mingle with the humans, who are much more than what the fey first believe. They are beings born without any type of magic. Beings who survive the lands, respecting it as the fey do. The fey learn from them and soon find themselves living in villages with the humans and taking human spouses.

The powers from the fey's homeland fades, and only their half-fey children survive the loss.

Underground, the dark fey thrive with the source's magic. Memories of the sun and life above ground have disappeared.

The men set out on a large hunt for meat. They plan to use the skins for clothing and bedding, for they have nothing. The deer they slay and consume morphs into something dark and rises again. But this time when it stands, it howls.

CHAPTER SEVEN

THE POWER IN THE CRYSTAL PUSHED MY FINGER AWAY, releasing me from the vision. My stomach clenched nauseatingly, and I swallowed down the bile that wanted to rise.

I looked at Drav in disoriented shock. His features, though darker, were the same as the man who'd picked the fruit. The same as the man who'd first touched the crystal. All the pieces fit together in my head, and the resentment over his callous disregard of my freedom of choice seemed insignificant in comparison to what had been taken from him.

He didn't understand the situation like I now understood it. He'd brought me underground because he truly believed this was a place of safety. Instead, it was a prison. His people had put him here because he and his friends had differing opinions. That wasn't even the worst part. They'd taken his memories. Everything. He'd stolen me to save me. But, his people had stolen from him because he saw the world differently.

"Mya?" Drav said softly.

His concerned gaze traced my face.

"I'm so sorry," I said a moment before I flew at him.

He caught me in his arms and held me tight. His cheek pressed against the top of my head, and he breathed in deeply, running his hands down the curve of my spine.

"You have no reason for sorrow. I told you, I accept and understand your anger."

I pulled back and looked up into his odd eyes. Eyes that had once been blue like the sky. Eyes that had changed as he'd adapted to his life underground.

"I'm not sorry for being mad at you. What you did is wrong. And I still want you to take me back to the surface. But Drav, I saw you and your people when I touched the crystal. I saw what you don't remember."

He frowned.

"What do you mean?"

"Before you came here, you lived in a forest. The trees were bigger than any building I'd ever seen. There was magic in that place, but it was dying. That's why you came here. At least, I think it was here, to the states. It was so long ago it's hard to tell, and the magic in these caves seems to warp distance or something. It would explain the hellhounds in Germany. Oh, the hellhounds! Drav, those were once deer."

"Yes. That is why we cannot eat the deer." The look in his eyes softened, and his hand brushed over the length of my spine. "I'm sorry I could not give you that."

I struggled not to shiver and to stay on topic.

"No way. Don't be sorry. Had I seen that thing pop back up with glowing red eyes and an attitude that I was prey, I would have been mad you hadn't warned me."

"What else did you see?" he asked, tenderly trailing his knuckles over my cheek.

"When you first came to the caves, you had pale skin and eyes lighter than a blue daytime sky." I reached up and ran my fingers over one of his braids. "You all wore your hair in braids like this. And your clothes blended with nature." With his caresses distracting me too well, I let my hands smooth over the material covering his shoulders. His muscles twitched under my touch and a hint of desire flared to life inside me.

I stepped back from him, putting some much-needed space between us so we focused on more important things than how good it felt to be touched by him.

"Drav, your people trapped you down here. They disagreed with your use of the crystals, but that didn't stop them from combining their power with that of the crystals they'd stolen. They used that power to curse the deer here, take your memories, and cause a cave-in. A very long time ago, you had a life before these caves. As much as what they did was a dick move, it also saved you."

The words struck a chord in me. I'd had a life before these caves, too. Drav taking me down here was a dick move. But, what if he really had saved me by doing so? I immediately rejected the similarities between what his people had done to him and what he'd done to me.

"When the magic of their world died, so did they. Well,

the original ones died. The kids they had with us humans continued to live on the surface just fine."

He remained silent for a moment.

"Do you understand what that means? You aren't meant to be down here, just like me. We're meant to go back, Drav. To the surface."

Before he could answer, someone spoke from behind him. I peeked around his side and saw the rest of the men standing on the path, bathed in the crystal's light, their clothes bloodier than before. Despite the gore clinging to them, they all seemed unharmed.

"How long was I touching the crystal?" I asked Drav.

"Not long." He turned to look at the other dark fey.

"The source did not give her a life crystal."

They seemed troubled by the news.

"I don't understand why that's so important to you, Drav."

"When we wear our crystal, we are safe. You need one."

I didn't see how he thought the crystals kept him safe. Maybe because of the weak light that those things cast? They sure hadn't seemed to provide any extra protection from the hellhounds just now. I didn't point any of that out, though.

"Maybe the source didn't give me a life crystal because I'm not meant to connect with its power the way you guys do. You possessed magic to start with. Even though I'm some kind of descendant, I never have. So, maybe it wouldn't have worked on me, anyway. Like I said, the magic of the world died out a long time ago. Well, everywhere but here."

Kerr said something while Drav continued to study me. Finally, he grunted in agreement.

"We need to go to the city, Mya. We only have a short time before the hellhounds return."

Because of the vision, I now had an idea of what that meant. Apparently, dead things didn't like staying dead down here. A shiver of fear travelled my spine. Drav must have seen it. He cupped the back of my neck and drew me forward, pressing his forehead against mine.

"I will keep you safe."

"But, why go to the city now? I just told you that you came from the surface, which happens to be the very same place I belong. The place you took me from against my will."

I pulled back, but he didn't look the least bit affected by my attempt at guilting him.

"We need to share what we've learned. Here and above," he said.

"And after that?"

"We will decide together."

The answer sounded reasonable, but I knew a covert "no" when I heard one. I didn't throw a fit, though. I'd learned my lesson from the last one. Instead, I decided to play nice for the moment. Fighting didn't work with Drav. I needed to figure out a way to convince him the surface was the best place for both of us. And fast.

"Ok. Thank you."

He moved to pick me up, and I stopped him.

"I feel bad that you have to carry me all the time. Would

it be easier if I hung onto your back or maybe if the others took turns carrying me?"

Several of the men said, "I carry Mya," at the same time, which started a new thought. Maybe I could convince one of—

Drav growled and turned to face the rest of the men.

"No one carries Mya but me."

I cocked my head at him, trying not to be annoyed.

"Drav, I only suggested it so you wouldn't get tired. I'm not a bone to fight over."

He turned back to me, a fierce light in his eyes.

"I swore to you I would not share you again. Ever."

He had me there. I sighed and gave in, wrapping my arms around his neck when he bent to lift me. The other men made comments in their language, but Drav ignored them as he started forward.

"What are they saying?" I asked.

"They want to know if you have friends."

I laughed. Species didn't change some things. My humor quickly died as I thought of Kristin and wondered if she'd made it to Irving. I hoped not. It had been a wasteland.

"Why are you sad?" Drav asked, studying my face.

"I used to have friends. I don't know if I still do. I need to find out, Drav. How long will it take to get me back home?" A desperate note crept into my voice despite my intention to play it cool.

"We will see what Molev has to say."

He looked forward, following the three men who led the way from the cave.

I settled in his arms, idly brushing my fingers against the back of his neck as I considered what waited for me at the city. Drav turned his head to look down at me, and the fingers of his hand supporting my lower half started to tease the skin of my thigh. I quickly stilled my movements and looked back at the three men traveling behind us. Each of their gazes flicked to me before returning to their study of our surroundings. I no longer resented their interest or curiosity. I couldn't begin to imagine what their lives had been like here.

AFTER HOURS OF RUNNING, we took a small break. Half the men left to fish at a nearby spring while another one took my water bottle to refill. I'd only surrendered it after he promised to fill it upstream from everyone. I didn't want to drink toilet water.

While the remaining two men and Drav lounged in the grass and conversed, I wandered through the protected grove. Even though I had Drav's assurance we were safe because of the light from the glowing crystals above, I didn't go far. I didn't need or want to. I only wanted a little space so I could think about everything the source crystal had shown me. A world of colossal trees and magic. A world of fey and dwarves and who knew what else. Despite experiencing the hellhounds and seeing people become zombies with my own eyes, the idea of there being even more to this new, upside-down world dumbfounded me. How had we forgotten so much of our history?

More importantly, why hadn't Drav seemed upset when I'd said his people had trapped him down here? I had no doubt he understood my words. However, I was beginning to doubt he understood the deeper meaning behind what I'd said.

His people had condemned all those who wanted to learn about the crystals to an eternity trapped in these dark caverns. For a people of earth and sky, that was essentially condemning them to living in hell. A hell that Drav was condemning me to, as well.

Yet, Drav and his friends had adapted. Maybe removing the memory of their time before the caverns had been a mercy, but anger still boiled inside of me on Drav's behalf. What if he'd had a family? The thought made my chest ache. I didn't want to disappear from mine like he had.

I glanced at him and found his watchful gaze on me. He stood and came my way, leaving one of his friends shaking his head.

"What's wrong?" he asked.

"Nothing."

"Why did you look so sad just now?"

"I was thinking about what happened to you. Why aren't you upset by the fact you were trapped down here?"

"Because I didn't feel trapped."

"Ever?"

He looked out at the trees for a moment.

"Ever. My oldest memories are of walking these caverns, learning to navigate them. It's a place of beauty. My home. I never wanted anything more until I met you."

His words made my heart jump and my guilt rise.

"Don't," he said, moving closer. He reached up and set his palm along my face, burying his fingers in my hair.

"Don't what?"

"Look at me with sorrow."

"You're right. I should be looking at you with annoyance. I haven't forgotten how you slapped my butt. I think I still have a handprint there."

He didn't say anything to that, only brushed his thumb over the skin of my cheek. I could see his regard for me in his gaze, and I struggled with what I felt in return. Before he'd brought me down here against my will, I would have said that what I felt crossed the line of mild interest. Okay, fine, what I felt leapt over the mild interest line. But now, I didn't know if it should.

Taking a breath, I decided to be honest. After all, Drav had no experience dealing with the opposite sex and likely no idea why what he'd done was wrong.

"I get that you forced me down here because you care and you want to keep me safe," I said, holding his gaze. "But knowing that you tricked me, that you took the choice to return to my family from me, hurt. It's like a lie, Drav. I need you to try to understand what you did. How would you feel if you were in my place? If I was your family and someone took me away and you didn't know if I was alive or dead?"

His thumb stilled.

"You are my family, Mya. And no one is taking you away from me."

The implied threat and his tone sent a shiver through me.

He saw it and cupped my head in his hands, setting his forehead to mine. I rested my hands on his arms, taking comfort in his touch.

"You are safe here, with me. I will not allow anything to happen to you."

"That's a big promise in a world going to shit."

He tipped his head and lightly brushed the tip of his nose against mine. His breath warmed my lips, and a tingle of awareness ran through me. My heart tripped. I swallowed hard and pulled back to meet his gaze, the move bringing our mouths closer. His fingers twitched in my hair, and his biceps tensed under my palms.

He wanted more. We both knew he did. And, the idea of using his affection to get my way again teased my mind. It would be so easy to tilt my head up just a bit further. What would it feel like to kiss him?

My lips parted. I wanted to try. And, not just to get my way. I tightened my grip on his arms. His breathing quickened as I started closing the gap.

Someone said something behind him, stopping me cold with the reminder that we had an audience.

Drav growled menacingly.

"You gotta stop growling in my face. I almost peed myself the last time you did."

He exhaled heavily, searched my gaze, then turned away from me to say something harshly in his language. I peeked around him and saw the others had returned. One caught my gaze and held out a leaf stacked with gelatinous globs of fish.

"Oh, thank you, but I'm more thirsty than hungry right now."

Drav turned on me.

"You need to eat."

"Maybe next year."

He frowned at me.

"Mya—"

"Drav, you spanked me and made me follow you into your scary-ass version of wonderland with rabid once-upon-a-time deer and face eating fish. If you make me eat when I'm telling you no, I'll make you wish you'd never been born. Got it?"

I felt bad about what had happened to him, but not bad enough to let him bully me.

He leaned close, intimidating me with his unblinking stare.

"Here we take threats as challenges. You will eat the next time we stop."

He turned away and took his portion of the fish before laying back down in the grass. Making a face at his closed eyes, I went to the man who was holding my water bottle and thanked him for filling it. I drained over half of it in an effort to drown the gnawing hunger in my belly. It wouldn't be too much longer before the raw fish started looking good. I put the water bottle away, and ignoring the knowing grins from the rest, I went and settled in next to Drav.

Wrapping his arms around me, he pulled me close. I shut my eyes.

A HOWL SPLIT THE AIR, and I jolted upright. Drav squatted beside me, putting a calming hand on my shoulder. He lifted a finger to my lips, an unnecessary warning to be quiet, then scooped me up into his arms. Exhaling shakily, I clung to him and watched the other men move silently, gathering their supplies and my bag.

Together, we ran through the grass, away from the howls.

"They won't come in here," Drav said against my ear as he ran. "Not until after the crystals dim."

"They dim?" My stomach dropped.

"Yes. Like your sun and moon, there is a night and day in most of the caverns. The crystals here will not dim for a while yet. We will have a lead."

A lead? That meant the hellhounds would follow us. I shuddered at the idea of being chased from one cavern to the next.

"How long until we get to the city?"

"Two more resting periods."

That didn't help me. I had no idea how long resting periods were or the time we spent running in between them. A watch would have been helpful. Briefly, I thought of my phone, but I didn't want to waste the battery. Without anything else to do, I settled into Drav's secure hold and listened to the slowly fading baying.

The dark fey moved swiftly, and Drav's steady pace carried us into the next, dimmer cavern. Knowing the hounds liked the dark and running into a space with less light after just hearing them didn't sit well with me. The men seemed to have the same thought because they increased their already fast pace.

"After we leave this area, we will rest again."

The greenery around us thinned and the ground slowly changed to dry, hard silt. Each of the men's steps kicked up dust in the semi-desolate area, leaving prints behind. Theirs weren't the only tracks I noted.

Huge paw prints covered the area. As I stared, the dull light seemed to fade even more. Maybe it was the dimming that Drav had spoken of earlier. I didn't really start to worry until it grew too dark for me to see ahead of us. The barely audible sound of the men's feet hitting the ground kept time with my racing heart.

How much of a lead did we have?

A distant howl echoed behind us, and I jerked my head to look over Drav's shoulder.

"Mya," he said, chiding me. "You are safe."

Kerr, who ran ahead of the group, picked up his pace and the others followed suit. Not comforting. Drav held me tighter and kept up.

"We are approaching our next resting spot," Drav said.

How could he even think of resting with the hounds somewhere behind us? And why didn't he even sound winded? My worry about him carrying me for too long seemed crazy, now. With the shadow men's ability to run, I wondered if they ever really needed to worry about the hellhounds. Even as I thought it, my mind flashed to our first encounter with the beasts, and I wondered what would have happened if one of them had caught us.

The thought sent a shiver down my spine.

"Are you cold, Mya?" Drav asked.

"I'm fine."

A lie I would keep telling myself until I believed it.

CHAPTER EIGHT

DRAV'S VERSION OF NOT LONG AND MINE WERE TWO VERY different things. The back of my knees and shoulders ached by the time the men started to slow.

The next cavern proved to be well-lit and lush with thick trees and wildlife. A bird took flight as we startled it from its perch. Distracted by the noise, I wasn't prepared when Drav suddenly leaned forward.

Startled, I gripped the back of his neck tightly and clung to him.

"We will stop soon, but I thought you would like to walk," he said, turning his head to look at me.

The realization that he'd been attempting to put me down barely registered. Our faces were only inches apart. Drav's exhale teased my mouth while his gaze held mine with an intensity and an awareness that robbed me of breath. Thoughts of home and caves fled with the slow heat that ignited in my stomach.

He inhaled slowly and whispered my name. His hands, set on my sides to steady me, smoothed up over my ribs, stilling just where his thumbs brushed the underside of my breasts. Nothing mattered more in that moment than discovering the feel of his lips against mine.

Unable to resist any longer, I set my hand against his jaw, my thumb stroking the tensed muscle there. He turned his head just enough to nip the pad of my thumb. The flickering fire in my belly grew.

Tilting my head up, I inched closer until our lips were barely an inch apart.

"Take me home, Drav," I breathed before moving to close the distance.

Someone spoke from behind me before our lips met. Drav growled in annoyance. I wanted to do the same.

"It's okay," I said. "You're right. I could use a break."

With reluctance, Drav released his grip on me.

Bargain then kiss, I berated myself as I stepped away, stretching my legs.

It felt good to move around. Drav stayed close to my side, and the men once again spread out around us. This time, I determined the pace as we moved forward.

My bag, slung across Kerr's back, caught my attention. My stomach, which had been emitting increasingly louder growls, needed something in it. Although I desperately wanted to get my hands on my bag and my water bottle, I didn't want to call attention to my growling stomach.

Kerr turned slightly, a notched arrow poised to fly. I

followed his watchful gaze, half-expecting to see a hellhound, despite the light.

"If you only use your weapons for hunting, then why use them now?" I asked Drav.

"We must find food," he said, giving me a pointed look.

So much for hiding my hunger. He'd probably heard each growl.

"My hunger wouldn't be a problem on the surface," I said softly, not wanting to startle away whatever critters Kerr hoped to shoot.

"We need to reach my city first, Mya."

My gaze again sought out my bag where the four precious cans hid. So little food. If I knew how long it would take for us to get to the city and back to the surface, I'd consider sacrificing a can now. Without knowing, though, I needed to try to hold out. My stomach clenched in rebellion.

Kerr lifted a hand, and Drav clasped my arm, stopping me. A few of the men ahead of us dropped to a crouched position, their hands brushing against their quivers, readying arrows. One of the others, who had a spear, lifted the deadly tip.

Before I could ask what was happening, Kerr's arrow flew. It whistled through the air and landed with a meaty thump. The men in front of us relaxed as they stood again.

Kerr motioned to the closest man, who took off in the direction the arrow had flown. Instead of trailing after him, the group started forward, veering in a different direction. Drav nudged me to follow.

We hadn't gone too far when the fey who had run off returned with a jackalope hanging from his belt. Without stopping, he handed Kerr the cleaned arrow and joined the group.

The men remained alert. I didn't hear anything, but a couple of times the men startled me with a sudden change in direction. The next time an arrow flew without warning, I squeaked and jumped, bumping into Drav. He wrapped a protective arm around me and pressed me to his side as the hunter ran off to fetch his kill.

"It's okay," I said against Drav's chest. "I was just startled by the sudden movement."

He nodded, releasing me. We continued to walk with the others.

"Is it always this difficult to find food?"

"No, but we are still on the outskirts. This is hellhound territory, and the other animals tend to stay away."

"Is that why there are fewer and smaller trees in these caves? Because we aren't closer to the source crystal?"

"No. The source crystal doesn't control all the growth. Each cave's crystals control that. The trees grow best in the light of strong crystals." The tone he'd used to answer me seemed abrupt.

"Are you annoyed?"

Drav grunted, and a few of the men shot me looks.

"Because my talking is scaring away potential food?"

Drav gave me a matching look.

"I'll take that as a yes."

"Mya, you need to eat. We need to hunt for that to happen. You must stay quiet," Drav said, not scolding, but I could see the worry in his eyes because I wasn't eating.

At the thought of food, my stomach growled loudly and my head throbbed. My gaze found its way back to my bag and the water that remained.

"One last question…will we be resting soon?"

"I will carry you," Drav said, misunderstanding the reason behind my question.

A couple of eager, 'I will carry, Mya' comments followed.

I shook my head, both at the willing men and Drav's offer.

"I'm good."

We walked through the knee-high, dusky purple grass growing between the pale blossoming trees. Grasping the passage of time or distance in this place proved too hard, and I gave up trying. Instead, I focused on the abundant plants and the way the grass squished underneath my feet.

While Drav remained beside me, the other men moved more swiftly through the trees, often disappearing from my sight for a minute before emerging. They seemed so at ease here that, although I felt bad for all they had lost, I could tell they had found the home they had searched for. Even as cruel as their home could be.

When the men finally slowed a few minutes later, I saw dead jackalopes hanging from most of their belts. One even had a bird. The men walked over a patch of grass, flattening it down, then unhooked their kills and set them in the middle.

"We will make camp here," Drav said, tamping down an area of tall grass for a sleep nest just off the main circle.

The fey brought out small skinning knives and started to work on their kills. My empty stomach turned at the sight, and I frowned. Under normal circumstances, I didn't think myself a squeamish person when it came to food prep. Hunger was messing with me. How long had we been down here already? Almost two days? And only a raw piece of fish to eat during that time.

I plopped down in the space Drav had created. He sat beside me and brushed the backs of his fingers along my arm. The touch comforted me, his need for constant contact not bothering me in the least.

Kerr came over, handed me my bag and Drav a jackalope. I immediately opened the bag, ignoring Drav's work, and dug inside for the water, which I sipped carefully. That action only added to a new urgent need, and I pressed my legs together.

"Drav…"

Hands full of jackalope innards, he paused to glance at me.

"Is it safe around here?"

"I will protect you."

"I know, but if someone had to take a quick walk, would it be safe?"

Drav stared at me, obviously confused. I leaned close, my lips just about to brush his ear.

"I have to pee," I whispered.

"I will take you," he said gently.

I wanted to groan because I didn't need company, just the assurance something wouldn't attack me with my pants down. Drav handed his jackalope to the closest man, who took it with a nod. The others continued their work as we walked away.

After relieving myself, my stomach cramped painfully with the need for food.

The subconscious hope I held for something resembling fried chicken died when we returned and I saw raw meat laying on a large frond in the center of their circle. It didn't escape my notice that the men hadn't yet touched the meat they had so carefully cut into strips. There could only be one reason for that. That shit tasted as bad as it looked.

Drav sat smoothly and waited for me to join him. Reluctantly sitting, I glanced at the meat. Drav picked up a few pieces and tried to hand them to me.

"You're not going to cook that?"

"The kill is fresh, and the meat still warm."

My brain gagged on that thought, and I picked up my water bottle, shaking it at him.

"I'm good."

"No, you must eat."

"I'm really okay. Seriously. You guys eat up."

"I warned you, Mya. You will eat."

I glanced at the bloody meat that Drav was offering. If I ate raw meat from a demon-eyed rabbit, I'd be lucky if the only thing I got was a tapeworm. With the world up top going to hell, I couldn't take the chance.

"Don't try bullying me. I'm not the one running around

carrying another person or fighting hellhounds. You guys have to keep your strength up. I will be fine."

Drav let out a slow breath, and I realized I'd really annoyed him. Good. I owed him.

"If you will not eat this," he said, "you will eat your food." He glanced meaningfully at my bag.

I followed his gaze, beyond tempted. Yet, worry still niggled the back of my mind. My stomach growled loudly.

"Your stomach agrees that you need food."

"It's a liar."

"Mya."

The warning tone of his voice didn't allow for argument. Not that I had any. Or willpower. I dug into the bag and pulled out a can of green beans. Thankful for the pull tab, I took the top off and tucked the metal circle back inside my pack. Drav and the others watched in fascination as I poured out the brine and fished out a piece.

I lifted the green bean to my lips. He shadowed my move with the piece of meat he held, the message clear. He wouldn't eat until I did. Rolling my eyes, I popped the bean into my mouth and chewed. He nodded and bit into the meat. The rest dug into their portions.

The quick, quiet meal of beans settled my angry stomach. Content, I scooted back a few steps and curled on my side. Drav settled in next to me.

Sleep tugged at me but not before I felt his lips brush against my forehead then my cheek.

Too bad we were surrounded by other people.

THE UNEXPECTED FEELING of my body leaving the ground penetrated my peaceful slumber. Before I fully woke, though, the press of Drav's forehead to mine and the firm hold of his arms reassured me. I became aware that we were moving again, but I didn't open my eyes. Cradled in his arms, I couldn't resist the temptation of sleep.

I roused again when Drav's arms tightened around me, his muscles rolled with his impressive pace. I'd just opened my eyes to see what had him moving so quickly when the desolate call of a hellhound echoed around us. Dread coated my mind.

"We are close to the next crystal source," Drav said, noticing I had woken up.

Looking around, I saw no welcoming glow of light.

The rhythmic sound of thumping feet grew louder behind us. When I peeked over Drav's shoulder, I saw the three dim blue lights from the feys' bracelets. Further back, I saw two sets of red eyes rushing toward us.

"Shit."

The men running behind us fell back to meet the attack. I watched the dim blue glow of their lights as they clashed with the hounds. The thwang of arrows and the thump of them hitting their marks echoed around us. After a grunt and a yip, one of the hounds fell behind, its eyes still glowing and moving slightly. Whatever the fey had done had stopped it, but not killed it. Just like on the surface, nothing seemed to kill the hounds.

The other set of red eyes neared one of the men, and I saw the lunging hellhound clamp down on his arm. Teeth dug into flesh. The fey grabbed the hound's snout with his free hand and pulled back almost as Drav had all those nights ago. The other two fey hovered close. As soon as the first fey pulled free of the beast's teeth, one of the men jumped on the hound, slitting its throat with a small blade.

The hound fell to the ground, not dead, but struggling to breathe and to get up again. The men left it and caught up with the group. Drav shifted my weight in his arms and ran faster.

The injured hound's noise began to fade with distance.

"Shouldn't we bandage him?" I asked, looking pointedly at the one with the injured arm.

"No. We must leave this area before the hounds heal."

My gaze returned to the wounded fey. He ran with the rest, seemingly unbothered by the blood coating his arm. If the hound's bite affected them as it did humans, the others would have been more upset. Right?

Just like before, the terrain changed slowly with the approach of another lit cavern. The barren ground gave way to short, sparse grass then wispy ferns.

A shiver shook me when we crossed from cool, dry air to humid warmth. The crystals' soft glow from above pulsed. Drav moved quickly and the sights flew by. Glimpses of trees with thick, broad drooping leaves and of vines twining up the rocky pillars teased me. A few times, I thought I saw a flower or colorful piece of fruit.

The group stopped after several minutes, and Drav slowly set me on my feet.

"We will rest for a bit, but we must leave before the crystals dim."

Drav's words about the crystals dimming during their version of night came back to worry me. The hellhounds would follow the scent of the wounded fey's blood.

I glanced at the man, who stood not far away, wiping at his wound with a huge leaf. Blood still smeared his arm. I moved toward Kerr.

"Can I have my bag, please?"

Kerr looked over my shoulder, where Drav hovered, before handing it to me. I took my bag and went to the wounded fey. With interest, he watched me approach.

"What's your name?" I asked.

The man glanced behind me before answering.

"Shax."

"May I look at your arm?"

Shax looked over my shoulder once more. This time I turned to glance at Drav, too. Drav met my gaze then nodded at Shax.

"Seriously? What do you think I'm going to do?" I said with an arched a brow. Drav didn't comment.

Turning back to Shax, I examined the arm he held out for my inspection. The blood ran darkly over the jagged bite. When I looked up to check Shax's eyes for any hint of cloudiness, he stared at me with unblinking focus.

"Let me know if you start craving human brains, okay?"

Not expecting an answer, I dug into my bag and pulled out my half-empty water bottle. Damn. Not cool, but I knew the wound needed to be cleaned. Wetting a large white bandage from my first aid kit, I gently washed away the clotting blood. The wound looked less horrifying once cleaned.

The others crowded around us, watching as I pulled out another bandage to wrap around his arm. Drav stopped me.

"He will be fine," he said.

"It should be covered so it doesn't get dirty."

"Save the wrap. He will be fine."

Drav gave Shax a look, and Shax nodded once before walking away without the bandage. I watched him pluck a new leaf and wrap it around his wound.

"He could have had the bandage," I said, turning to look at Drav. "There are more of them."

"He does not need it, but you may."

A frustrated groan escaped me.

"If you really think that, then why am I down here? Wasn't the point because it's supposed to be safer? Just take me home, Drav. Let the rest go to the city."

"We go together.

Frustrated, I turned away from him and started to put my things away. Immediately, I noticed my water bottle missing. I checked the nearby plants in case the empty bottle had rolled. However, I didn't find it. Panic began to grow. Without the water bottle, how would I drink? Stuff in the water wanted to eat my face.

Drav said nothing as he watched my increasingly frantic search.

One of the other men approached and said my name, interrupting my efforts. Glancing up with impatience, I saw my filled water bottle in his hand. Relief coursed through me.

"Thank you." I stood and accepted the cold container.

"Upstream," he said with a smile.

I grinned in return and put the bottle away. Kerr came for my bag, and I noticed the crystals certainly had dimmed during our short break.

"Did you need to go pee?" Drav asked.

"I'm good."

"I will only be gone for a moment. The others will watch over you."

After he relieved himself in the trees, we were on the move again. As we passed from cavern to cavern, I caught glimpses of beauty in this underground world. Different trees that spiraled versus growing straight and plant life that grew as tall and strong as the trees.

We emerged from a fertile cavern into a vast space which easily stretched for miles and had a ceiling so high the crystals twinkled like distant stars. In the distance, a larger crystal shown like a full moon on a clear night.

The men moved swiftly, their leather clad feet barely making a noise against the hard surface of this cavern's floor.

Awe filled me as I studied everything I could see. That awe turned to stunned disbelieve when I caught sight of a stone wall stretching beyond sight in both directions.

The closer we drew, details became clearer. The soft light

played on veins of white running through the gray and black stone that seamlessly rose out of the cave's floor. Carved out of existing stone, or made from magic, the wall was a part of the cave.

"What is this place?" I asked.

"Our city," Drav answered.

CHAPTER NINE

KERR PULLED AHEAD, OUTDISTANCING THE REST OF US.

"Where's he going?"

"To tell the others to open the door," Drav said.

"Door?"

Kerr's faint shout reached us, and I watched a figure appear near the top of the stone wall. A moment later, the figure waved an arm and disappeared again. A grating, low rumble filled the air and a crack emerged in the smooth expanse of rock just as Kerr reached the wall.

We joined him not long afterward, and I stared at the massive stone entrance before me.

The wicked, long furrows in the heavy slabs that comprised the entry to the city momentarily distracted me from what lay inside. When I did finally focus, shock filled me. The uninhabited, wild areas outside the wall had misled me into believing Drav's "city" would be nothing more than hovels grouped together in more of the same wild. I should have known better.

A dirt trail, bordered by thick flowering vegetation, wound its way toward a vast grove of trees towering high in the distance. In the immense space between the gate and the grove, neatly planted fields spread out to the right and left, illuminated by countless crystal lanterns suspended at the top of long poles. Soft, glittering lights gave the land a surreal feel.

"It looks like fairy lights," I said softly.

Drav jogged through the opening and deposited me on my feet. I felt him leave my side as I continued to look around.

They were farmers. Even with what the crystal had shown me, my mind struggled to process the concept of cave farming. Actual dirt lay beneath my feet, not stone. How?

I already knew the answer. The source had shown me that the magic to influence nature ran in their blood. The proof of what their powers, combined with that of the crystals, could accomplish stunned me. Not only had they created a wall, they'd created arable earth.

The grinding rumble of the gate drew my attention, and I turned around to watch Drav and another man strain to push the stone slab closed. Their muscles rolled and flexed with each laborious step.

"I wouldn't want that job. How many times a day do they need to open the gate?"

The gate closed with a rasping thud. Drav moved back to

my side as two men slid an enormous log into place to brace the stone slab.

"The gate is almost never used," Drav said. He pointed to a pair of tall ladders that leaned against the wall just inside the door. "We use the ladders. There is less chance of the hounds slipping in that way."

"Wow."

A group of new men stared at me from where they stood near the gate.

"Hello," I said before Drav could speak. "I'm Mya. I'm not a male like you, but a female from the surface."

Their eyes widened with sudden understanding, and they looked at me with even more interest while the men in our group sniggered and said a few words under their breaths.

"No, I'm not willing to show you my physical differences. No, you can't touch me. I'd prefer you not smell me, either. It makes me nervous and uncomfortable. I don't understand your language, but know you can understand me. I don't have a crystal or magic like you all do. Thank you for opening the gate and letting me in."

Speech given, I glanced at Drav and found him considering me.

"What?" I asked.

"They will all want to touch you and smell you no matter what you say."

"Then we're going to have problems, aren't we?"

He sighed and nodded as if it were a foregone conclusion, which I found unacceptable. I needed a deterrent. How did one discourage a city full of demon men who ripped off heads for fun?

"Would it hurt if I kicked you guys in the balls?" I asked.

He tilted his head and gave me a puzzled look. So did the rest. Slang didn't translate well.

"Your soft bits that hang between your legs. The two balls."

Understanding lit their gazes. Several of the men in our immediate group grunted and moved a little further away from me. Kerr chuckled and said something to Drav, who frowned.

"We don't kick there. Ever," Drav said, quite seriously.

"Well, I will if I'm touched or sniffed without permission." I glanced at the men. "You've been warned." I hoped I'd put some fear in them because that empty threat summed up the whole of my weak defense. Bigger, stronger, faster...they could overpower me at any time. I knew that. Deep down they probably did too.

"Are you ready?" I asked, changing the subject.

"Yes. It is safe for you to walk here. But, I would like to carry you so we can reach the city faster."

"Go ahead. I'm all for faster."

The words had barely left my mouth before Drav scooped me up. The men by the wall called out a word as the rest of our group started running down the path.

Drav didn't immediately move to follow as I expected, and I looked up to see why.

The expression he wore heated my cheeks.

"I've wanted this a very long time."

"What?"

"You here. Safe. Letting me hold you."

"But just to deliver the information and go, right?"

Our gazes locked, and his fingers brushed my ribs near my breast.

"Maybe you should focus on running instead of me."

"I'm always focused on you, Mya. Especially when I'm running with you in my arms. I like the way you jiggle."

My mouth dropped open.

"I do not jiggle," I said indignantly.

He took off, sprinting down the trail, and his gaze dipped to my chest. I followed the direction of his focus and rolled my eyes at the sight of my ever so slightly bouncing boobs.

"That is barely a jiggle. You made me sound like a bowl of Jell-O."

"I think I might enjoy Jell-O."

I snorted. "Probably."

Now that he'd pointed out his fascination, I paid more attention to him instead of the landscape. His eyes did indeed repeatedly return to my chest.

"You really do have a thing for boobs, don't you?"

"Yes. They look interesting when you are undressed, and they feel so soft. I like when you sleep and let me hold them."

"Wait a minute. Sleeping isn't permission to hold them. It just means I'm not conscious to object."

"Yes. I like that."

His ignorance kept him safe from me slugging him.

"How would you like it if I waited until you slept and grabbed your balls really, really hard?"

He frowned for a moment, and I realized he was considering it.

"Seriously, Drav? The point is that you wouldn't like me doing stuff to you while you slept, so you shouldn't do it to me."

"I might like it. Your hands are soft and gentle. You're not as strong. It might not hurt so much."

I groaned and looked away from him for a moment, trying to think of a way to help him understand.

"Do you understand the concept of stealing?" I asked, looking up at him.

"Yes. Stealing is forbidden here."

"It's forbidden where I'm from, too. When you touch me without my agreement, it's like stealing from me. I need to give my approval for the touches to mean something. It's supposed to be special, Drav."

"It is special," he said, looking troubled.

"If I haven't agreed to it, it's only special to you, not me. Do you understand?"

"Yes." He stared ahead for a long while.

I checked the path and could barely see his friends further ahead.

"When will you give me your permission?" Drav asked, drawing my attention again.

Not will you, but when will you. His confidence amazed me.

"If you don't take me back to the surface, I might not ever give it," I said with an arched brow.

He grunted and focused on the path for a long while. I

smothered a grin at the tightness in his jaw and turned away to watch the grove.

Even though the view of the forest grew larger, the distance to reach it never seemed to change. With each field we passed, I began to wonder just how big the towering trees would be. I had to admit more than a mild curiosity filled me when I began to see tiny specks of light within the inky tops.

Given the size of the cavern, I could understand the need for the field lanterns and the ones in the trees. The wall stretched out so far, I lost sight of it. Not only was the area hard to light, but how could they possibly guard the whole thing?

"Have they ever gotten in? The hellhounds?"

"A few times. But we return them back to where they belong."

"How do you know when they get in? This place is huge."

"The outlying villages guard the walls. If any hounds do manage to climb over, the light of the crystals in the fields hurt them, and they make plenty of noise to let us know where they are."

When I turned back to the grove, I could finally make out the shapes of the outer most trees, which seemed small in comparison to the central ones. Drav's reason for wanting to carry me became clear. What I'd thought a distant, normal grove of trees was turning out to be a forest of the largest trees I'd ever seen.

"Just how tall are those trees?" I asked.

"I do not know. Very tall."

Details became clearer, and I realized just how giant the

massive trees were. They towered high above, their inky leaves almost touching the vast cavern's soaring top and kissing the crystals inlaid there.

Entering the shadows of the trees, I saw what Drav's people had done. Without even knowing it, they'd recreated the home of their ancestors. The home they'd been sent to find. My eyes watered, and Drav noticed. He slowed to a walk.

"Why are you crying? Are you afraid? I will keep you safe."

I leaned my head against his chest and put my hand over his heart.

"I know you'll keep me safe. And, I'm not crying exactly. Just emotional. Girls do that sometimes."

He grunted and held me a little closer, leaning his head in to smell my hair and nuzzle my neck. A tingle of awareness shivered through me.

"Is it all right if I walk for a while?" I asked.

"Yes." He set me on my feet and held out his hand. I threaded my fingers through his and walked by his side, marveling at our surroundings.

"You brought seeds with you into the caves," I said, sharing what the source crystal had shown me. "I think these are seeds from the trees of your homeland. Trees that were dying. I think that your people's magic was connected to the forest's magic somehow. When the magic faded from the surface, so did theirs. But not here. Maybe because the crystal helped feed the magic of the trees. Your magic."

We came to one tree that had vines twisting up its ancient

bark. Large, white, bell-shaped flowers drooped from thin shoots. The fragrant air tickled my nose, and I gave in and inhaled deeply. The intoxicating smell wrapped around me, seeming to sooth away all my travel aches.

I inhaled again, appreciatively.

"It's like a fairytale in here," I said. "So pretty."

"Careful. The scent of that plant can be very relaxing."

"Really?"

"Yes. We use it for healing and celebrating."

The image of a bunch of men standing around and smelling flowers filled my head and I giggled. I could picture Drav with one in his hair and Kerr asking to sniff it. I snorted hard, and a laughing fit had me bending over in near tears.

Suddenly, the world spun, and Drav was carrying me again at a run.

"Too much fieayla flower for you."

It took a few minutes for my head to stop spinning and for the laughter to settle down.

"That stuff is strong." I leaned my head against his shoulder and looked around at the trees. "I hope that's not growing in the city."

"No. We keep it to the outer trees."

A glimmer of lights in the treetops caught my attention. I squinted, trying to determine if I was seeing through the canopy or if someone had placed crystal lanterns in the trees.

"Are there lanterns up there?" I asked.

"Yes. To mark every home."

"Home?"

Drav stopped running and looked up at the tree.

"Welcome to Ernisi, our city."

I blinked, feeling quite Drav-like, and looked around at the empty forest floor then at the towering canopy. There was nothing here. When he'd said city, I'd kept imagining a bustling underground metropolis. That's not what I saw. I saw a quiet forest.

On my second sweeping glance, I glimpsed a set of stairs cleverly created out of curled pieces of massive bark.

"Holy shit," I said for the second time.

Drav smiled slightly and started for the nearest tree. He took the steps at an easy-for-him run. My stomach plummeted at how quickly we ascended and at how very tall the tree rose and at how no railing existed on the not too wide stairs.

I squeezed my eyes shut and focused on my breathing.

Several minutes later, Drav slowed.

"You can look, Mya."

I opened my eyes and saw we stood on a massively wide branch. The abnormally flat surface created a roadway that stretched out far from the trunk of the tree. Smaller branches, wider than an RV, protruded from the main branch, along with enormous burls.

Nearby, men stood gathered before a hut carved out of the first burl on the main trunk. A lone man stood on a raised part of the burl, giving him height and making it easy for him to see out over the crowd and for the crowd to see him. His gaze locked on us.

"Who is that?" I said softly.

Drav eased me to my feet.

"That is Molev."

Even without the help of the burl, the dark fey stood a bit taller than Drav. He, like all the other men, wore his black hair in tight, masculine braids that gave him a Viking look. His face seemed vaguely familiar. One of the original ten.

Molev stared at me with the same curiosity as the others had. The crowd of men noticed his regard and turned to look at us. The numerous gazes pinned me, and the urge to repeat my speech from earlier arose.

Molev spoke, reclaiming the men's attention.

"Who is he to your people?" I whispered.

"Our leader."

Molev continued to speak to the men in Drav's language.

"What is he saying?"

"He is telling the group what happened to Phusty."

"Oh."

I glanced at Drav and saw the hopelessness in his expression. A sweeping urge to offer him some sort of comfort had me clasping his hand and giving it a gentle squeeze.

"I'm really sorry."

The guy hadn't been nice, but according to the crystal, Drav had known him a very, very long time.

Drav gave a minute nod, and the longer he listened to Molev, the more his lips tightened. A figure broke away from the group and came toward us. Ghua's frown matched Drav's. When he reached us, they spoke in quiet tones. The more Ghua said, the more Drav looked pained.

"What's wrong?" I asked.

"Phusty has not come back."

"They lost his body?"

"No. He did not return to the waters," he said.

I opened my mouth to ask what he meant, but Molev spoke loudly, recapturing my attention. Whatever he said had the men dispersing. As each passed us to descend the stairs, they gave me a good once over. No one stopped to speak with Drav, though. I glanced at Molev and found him watching me. His gaze shifted to Drav, and he tilted his head to indicate the burl.

Drav touched the small of my back, and Drav, Ghua, and I joined Molev inside. Several small lanterns filled with crystals lit the interior of the burl. The soft glow danced on the smoothly carved walls curved to allow for seats and a built-in bed around the perimeter. Stepping closer, I studied the swirls in the woodgrain of the stunning walls and ran a finger along a curve. With that one touch, I understood that no carving tool had created this place. Magic had.

Molev spoke a stream of words while looking at Drav. Hearing Phusty's name mentioned a couple of times, my worry grew not only for Drav but for myself.

"Phusty had his crystal on him," Drav said when the man quieted.

Molev spoke some more and Drav responded.

"He challenged me for the right to study Mya. We fought. I won. He did not return. Ghua and the others brought him here, thinking that might change."

Molev turned his attention to Ghua and seemed to ask him a question.

"The waters did not mehornan. He had his crystal on him," Ghua said.

The mix of their language and English didn't help me understand anything.

"What's the big deal with his crystal?" I asked, trying to piece together their conversation.

"The life crystal we wear protects us from death," Drav said.

"Yeah, you mentioned it keeps you safe."

"Not just safe. I don't know the right word, but when we wear the crystal, we don't have a real death."

All the little things Drav had been trying to explain finally clicked into place. They didn't have death because the crystals brought them back to life. Like the deer in the vision.

"That's why you wanted to get me a crystal," I said slowly.

Drav stepped up to me and pressed his forehead against mine. The caring of this man made my heart race.

"It wasn't just protection. You didn't want me to die."

"You are safe here. Even without the crystal."

"Safe, but not staying, right?"

His thumbs brushed across my cheekbones, and I wrapped my fingers around his wrists, holding him in return.

"Safe," he repeated.

Drav took a step back, and I released my hold on his wrists. Ghua and Molev were watching us closely. I cleared my throat, feeling awkward under their curious gazes.

"Drav, Ghua," Molev said. The string of words that followed had the two nodding as they listened.

My thoughts drifted to Phusty's death and the men's reactions. When Drav ripped off his head, none of them had batted an eye. After a few minutes, though, they'd nudged the fallen man with their feet and had argued. It all made sense, now. They'd expected Phusty to get back up. The idea of it boggled me. Sure, I'd seen it in a vision, but the deer had come from the caves and...I recalled the way the men in the vision had brought the deer outside, and my stomach sank. They couldn't resurrect outside this place.

"There haven't been any traces of them yet," Drav said, interrupting my thoughts.

Molev glanced at Ghua, who shook his head. I frowned as I listened. Molev paced, speaking again.

"It is possible that they were attacked by the hounds on the surface," Drav said.

Molev nodded but waved his hands angrily as he spoke a clipped smattering of words.

"Good that they stay on surface," Ghua interjected.

"Who?" I asked.

Molev spoke over my question and Drav answered him, ignoring me.

"We've had guards on the entrances. Someone would have seen if they had returned."

Molev calmed at that and stared into space. He directed his next words at Ghua, who nodded and left the room.

"What's happening?" When Drav didn't immediately answer, I poked him. "What the hell is going on?"

"We didn't only go to the surface for exploration. Long ago, two of our people did something unthinkable. They killed another after taking his crystal. Without his crystal, he did not return. It is an unforgivable act. The men were exiled and forced to live outside the city walls."

I glanced at Molev then focused on Drav.

"Are you going to be exiled?" I asked.

"No. I did not know what would happen on the surface. Phusty wore his crystal. He should have returned."

"So what's the big deal about the two who were exiled? Why's he so upset?" I glanced at Molev who listened patiently.

"When the hole opened, we believe they fled with the hounds. They went to the surface."

CHAPTER TEN

Pieces of their conversation made scary sense now. Ghua wanted the criminals to stay on the surface because the fey could die a real death up there. However, he was only thinking of this world's safety, not mine. What chance did humanity have against two powerful fey who didn't care if people came back or not?

"You can't leave them up there. We have to go back, now, to find them and to find my parents."

"No, Mya. It is too dangerous."

"It's too dangerous for every uninfected human if those two stay up there."

"Mya."

"No," I said, stepping away from him. "We came to your city and shared the information like you said. Now, you keep your promise. You said we would decide together. Telling me it's too dangerous sounds a hell of a lot like you're trying to decide for me, not with me."

"Mya..." He stalked me, backing me to a wall.

My gaze snapped to his, and I saw the worry there.

"Molev has commanded everyone to return below. Ghua is heading out now to share the news."

"What? Why didn't you say that sooner? He could have taken me with him." I looked at the door, wondering if I could catch Ghua.

"I said I would not share," Drav said with a growl.

"Going with Ghua isn't sharing. He could have taken me back home. Like I want. Like I've been begging you to do since the moment you tossed me over your back, you ass."

"No."

"What do you mean no? You don't get to decide, Drav. I'm not one of you. Molev can't keep me here, and neither can you."

I slapped my hands to his chest, trying to push him away. Instead, he caught my hands and leaned in, his expression fierce.

"Don't forget, Mya. Your people are destroying the surface to kill the infected. To kill anything that is not human. They do not care if they kill healthy humans while doing so."

I scowled at him, hating he was right about that.

"Fine, my people are assholes. But so are yours. Just because your people can die on the surface, your leader is leaving the criminals and having the rest return without cleaning up the mess that you all created." A sudden thought stopped me cold, and I stared up at Drav in shock.

"Did you know that would happen? That once Molev found out you guys could die up there, he would command everyone to stay underground? Is it one of the reasons you brought me here? To trap me?"

"No. I said I would keep you safe. With the bombs up there, it is safer to wait down here. If the source would have given you a crystal and Phusty would have returned..." He sighed. "Please stay until it is safe for you to go home."

Like I had a choice without his help. We'd nearly died twice trying to reach the city.

A grunt sounded from behind Drav, a reminder we weren't alone. Drav released me and stepped to the side to face Molev. Molev studied me and spoke. Drav translated.

"He wishes to learn more of your words," Drav said. "You could give him the device you allowed me to use to learn your words."

I tightened my hold on my bag, which hung over my shoulder.

"Oh, that's not a good idea. Definitely no."

"Mya."

"No."

"He only wishes to be able to communicate with you in your language."

"I'm good with using you as a translator."

"It would be much easier for him to learn with the device."

There was no way I was going to give them the iPod with my mom's more scandalous reads on it. Perhaps I could delete them off. I would have to check later to see if that function existed. Until then, though...

"No," I repeated, more firmly.

Molev chimed in again, the look on his face thoughtful. Drav listened and nodded.

"We will discuss this later. Since we have travelled so far, Molev suggests we rest. Afterwards, there will be a feast so he can share the news about the surface."

Molev left the burl mid-explanation. Resting sounded amazing, but I couldn't stop thinking about Molev's decision.

"You mean about abandoning the surface?" I said as Drav led me out. "Drav, my family is still out there. I need to find them."

Drav remained quiet for a moment before halting me.

"I promise, Mya, when it is safe, we will return for them."

His words didn't reassure me. Who would determine when it became safe? I doubted the bombs would kill every infected or hellhound, and with them still present, Drav would want to keep me down here forever.

"When, Drav? Up top may never be safe again," I said. "And that's exactly why I need to go back. My family needs me, and you, if they're going to have any hope of surviving. I'm willing to compromise and give the bombing a few more days to settle down, but that's it. With or without you, I'll leave." Or at least I would try to. I really hoped it didn't come to that.

"Agreed." He said the word quickly and firmly, leaving me no doubt that he meant it. A few days was more than I wanted to give, but Ryan said they were in a safe zone, and they'd survived the first week. They would survive a few more days. They had to.

When Drav threaded his fingers through mine and gently

tugged me in the direction of the massive tree trunk, I begrudgingly followed.

"Are we going back down?"

"No. Up. We'll find an open home to rest."

"Open home? Don't you live here?"

"My home is in one of the outer villages. I only come to the city when called."

"You know, when you said city, I thought you meant something…more."

He glanced at me.

"What do you mean?"

"Are there any shops here? Or anything else besides homes?"

"No. We don't need anything more than somewhere to sleep."

"So all you do is farm and sleep?"

"No. We hunt and train, too."

When we reached the steps, he stopped.

"Do you want me to carry you up?"

I didn't bother to look up or down, just nodded.

Safely in his arms, I closed my eyes and concentrated on the wind on my face until he stopped again.

"It's quieter up here and not often used," he said.

I opened my eyes and found we stood on another wide branch. Wide by surface standards, but not as broad as the one Molev called home. Thankfully, no wind disturbed the branch or caused any swaying when Drav eased me to my feet.

"You may choose for us," he said, gesturing to the line of four burls.

"The one closest to the tree might be best." I moved toward the entrance, glad I didn't catch a view over the edge of the branch. I never had a fear of heights. To be fair, though, I'd never needed to be up so high without guardrails before.

The inside of the burl looked the same as Molev's. A natural bench curved from the wall and widened near the back. A depression near the door looked like a large empty basin, but other than that, the place was bare.

"There's not much here. Do you really do nothing else but sleep here?" I set my bag on the part of the bench near the door.

"Just sleep."

"The bed doesn't look very comfy."

He glanced at the wooden platform at the back and frowned.

"Your beds are softer," he agreed.

"Yeah. By a lot."

"You can sleep on me."

I glanced at him and saw he looked entirely serious. Warmth started in my face and spread in tingling waves throughout my body. We were alone and safe for the first time in days. My gaze drifted to his lips, and I couldn't deny I was tempted by his offer. Too tempted. If I gave in, he'd never want to take me home.

"Sleeping on you might not be a good idea."

"Why?"

Crap.

"If all you do is sleep in this room," I said, changing the subject, "where do you eat, bathe, go to the bathroom, and all the other stuff?"

"We do all of that on the ground. Why don't you want to sleep on me, Mya?"

"You're annoyingly persistent sometimes."

"I only want to understand." He stepped closer to me, crowding into my space. Lifting a hand, he trailed his fingers down my cheek.

"I want to understand why touching you like this makes me hurt right here." He captured my hand and laid it on his chest. At the contact, he closed his eyes. "I want to know if you like being touched by me as much as I like being touched by you." He opened his eyes to look at me. "I want to understand why it is not special to you when it means everything to me."

I swallowed with difficultly, trying hard to stifle the wave of heat that washed through me.

"It is special, now, when I'm awake. I only meant you shouldn't do stuff when I'm asleep."

"I won't touch your breasts or pussy. I will just hold you."

What the hell was I supposed to say to that?

"Uh, thanks. I'll think about it."

"Good." His fingers brushed over my skin once more then stilled as he continued to stare down at me. Several long moments passed.

"I didn't mean I'm going to think about it right now. I need some time to decide."

Disappointment clouded his expression before he exhaled heavily. He really wanted me sleeping on top of him. The idea of just how badly he wanted that had my insides dancing.

"Maybe you can show me around on the ground so I know where everything is. That feast Molev mentioned sounds interesting. Will there be something other than raw meat?"

"Yes. Are you hungry?"

"Maybe. It all depends on the food."

"Come. I will carry you below."

A few minutes later, I had my feet firmly planted on solid terrain, and we walked side by side under the giant trees. Rich dark soil covered the paths that wove through the random vegetation. Unlike the fields, everything in the forest felt naturally placed, like seeds in the wind. However, the longer we walked, the more I noticed subtle patterns.

"These weren't randomly planted, were they?"

"No. Plants for healing are grouped together. Plants for weaving are spread throughout, so the harvest doesn't empty one place. Plants to sweeten the air are used around bathroom areas as are the soft plants for cleansing. And, plants for washing are closer to the water."

"Wow. I guess you'll need to teach me a lot of plants. Especially the soft ones for cleansing. I don't want to mess that up with something else…you know, just in the few days we're going to be here."

He nodded and began to point out the different types. Their unique leaf patterns and the way the plants grew made them easily distinguishable from their neighbors, once I knew what to look for.

Before long, we stood at the edge of a large clearing. Stumps, like campfire seats, were scattered in an almost haphazard way around a huge central piece at least ten feet in diameter. About half the number of men from the earlier meeting walked about in the clearing. Some of them conversed in small groups, and some set down leaves covered with bits of something onto the communal table.

My stomach growled, and Drav nudged me forward. The murmur of male voices quieted as we approached, and it felt like every man present stared at me.

"Hello," I said, clearly. "My name is Mya. I'm not a male, like you, but a female from the surface. I don't like to be grabbed or touched or smelled. It makes me uncomfortable."

A low murmur spread throughout the gathered crowd. A few of the men approached us right away. They spoke to Drav but stared at me the entire time.

Drav repeated the story of finding me in a truck, accidently grabbing me, and discovering I had different parts. While I listened, I glanced around, mostly trying to see what kinds of food the newcomers were adding to what already waited on their table. The can of beans was just a distant memory, and my stomach made sure to let me know that with a steady stream of cramps and growls.

One man carried something past that looked like a stuffed cabbage roll. My mouth watered, and my feet decided we needed to follow. Drav didn't say anything when I stepped away. I could feel him watch me, though. However, everyone seemed to respect my little don't-touch-me message.

The man set his leaf on the table then walked away after giving me a once over. Stepping closer, I looked over the food already waiting. Most of it looked like raw meat, but a few things appeared to be some kind of fruit or vegetable. I even saw one of those flowers that had made me laugh. The best-looking dish, in my opinion, remained that cabbage roll looking thing.

My brain took a backseat as my stomach made the decision we needed to eat right then. Snatching up a roll, I had half of it in my mouth before anyone could stop me. The mouthwatering flavors burst upon my tongue as I chewed. The outside of the roll was some kind of leaf, and the inside seemed stuffed with a blend of meat and soft grain. Although probably uncooked, it still tasted like heaven.

Yelling exploded somewhere behind me, but I kept eating, not bothering to turn and look. Not even when I heard my name. My thoughts remained focused on the next roll I grabbed. The second roll caused more people to yell. I knew I should have felt bad that I'd started eating before the feast officially began, but I couldn't manage it. Instead, I chewed and groaned in bliss.

The arguing quieted, and it took a moment for it to click that everyone stared at me again. I swallowed and lifted the half-eaten roll.

"This is so good. I was starving."

Drav stepped away from the three men glaring at him and came to me. His tender expression swept over my face.

When he reached me, he cupped the back of my head and touched his forehead to mine.

My stomach did a tiny flip that had nothing to do with food and everything to do with the man smoothing his thumb over the skin near the corner of my mouth.

"Eat as much as you want," he said softly.

Grumbles and angry shouts erupted after that statement. Drav pulled away to face the crowd.

"Enough," he roared. The men quieted, some glaring at him. Some glaring at me. Most just watching everything.

"Mya's world is not like ours. They do not have the same customs. She is hungry, and I want her to eat."

I picked up another roll and took a bite to show I agreed. One of the glarers took offense and said something to Drav in angry tones.

"She does not have a life crystal. She isn't one of us to be challenged."

Whoa…what?

"What's going on?" I asked after swallowing my mouthful.

"Groi, Vair, and Limar are angry you ate before them. They believe they have the right to challenge you. However, it is not our way to challenge someone without a life crystal." He looked at the men when he spoke his next words. "I will accept challenges on Mya's behalf."

That didn't sound good. Worried, I glanced at the angry men, hunger forgotten. Two of them said something, continuing to look fierce. The third waved his hand and stepped back.

"Is anyone else offended?" Drav asked. No one came forward. "Good. We will go now."

The two men nodded and strode through the crowd in the direction opposite from where we'd arrived. Drav nudged me to follow.

"What exactly does a challenge mean?" I asked, nervously.

Drav threaded his fingers through mine as we walked the path out of the clearing.

"It means that I will fight Grio and Limar. May I carry you? We will get there faster."

"Yeah, sure, but—"

I was up in his arms then robbed of air as the sudden wind hit my face. Instead of trying to finish my thought, I turned my head into Drav's shoulder.

What the hell had happened? I'd eaten three dumb rolls out of a ton of food set out for everyone. It shouldn't have been a big deal, but apparently here, it was. I'd managed to offend them by eating first. I hadn't even considered it might be something more than just rude. I'd been so hungry I hadn't thought of anything else.

Drav stopped and put me down. Before looking around, I apologized.

"I should have asked. I wasn't thinking. I was just hungry."

Drav tenderly stroked my cheek.

"You did nothing wrong."

"Apparently I did, or we wouldn't be here."

Here turned out to be a large area of packed, barren

ground at the edge of the forest. A faint rumble caught my attention, and I turned my head to see water cascading from the craggy face of the far cavern's wall. A subterranean waterfall. Droplets of mist rose in the air, sparkling dimly from the few scattered crystals near the water's source.

"That's amazing," I said quietly.

"We will go there when I'm done with these two."

That drew my attention to the two men standing in the center of the clearing. Both waited, shirtless and facing us.

"You're fighting both of them?"

"Yes."

"Like how you and Ghua fought, right?"

"No, Mya."

My stomach dropped as I remembered Drav's fight with Phusty. The intense struggle between the two of them would have upset me more had I known someone would end up without a head.

The idea of Drav fighting like that now terrified me. Yes, I understood that Drav thought the crystal would keep him safe, but I'd seen what had happened to the deer they'd taken outside in the vision. It hadn't come back. What if, when he'd gone up to the surface, he'd weakened whatever connection he had with his crystal? What if going to the surface had broken it?

I couldn't think like that. Drav had overcome Phusty. He would win this challenge, too. No problem. I glanced over his shoulder at his opponents. Both men looked fierce and strong, and they each closely matched Drav in size.

"You're facing them one at a time, right?"

"No."

Panic bubbled up inside me.

"That's not fair."

"It is how we settle arguments." He pulled off his shirt and tossed it to one of the men behind us.

Two fey wanted to fight him at the same time because of a dumb cabbage roll? How could he be so casual about this?

"Kerr, stay with Mya."

With that, Drav started to walk away.

"Wait." I grabbed his hand, and he turned back to me.

Standing on my toes, I wrapped my arms around his neck. He leaned in and set his forehead against mine. His steady green gaze swept over my features as I shook with fear for him. I couldn't survive in this new world alone. I needed him. He needed to win this.

His arms circled around me, giving me comfort and adding to my desperation.

"Come back safe. Please."

Before I could second guess myself, I pressed my lips to his.

He jerked slightly, then growled softly. One hand slid down to my butt, gripping me and lifting me while the other cradled the back of my head. My breasts flattened against the bare expanse of his chest. The contact sent a shiver through me, and I made a small sound.

With another growl, he licked my parted lips. I gasped, giving him the entrance he sought. His hot tongue swept over mine without hesitation. He wanted, and he took. Heart thundering, I slid my fingers into his hair and lost myself to the sensation of his lips against mine.

Someone nearby yelled something. Drav pulled back. While I gasped for breath and struggled to think clearly, he set me down and put his forehead to mine.

"Thank you, Mya." He released me and walked toward the waiting men.

I blinked at his chiseled back. My lips felt swollen and tingly. The brief, passionate kiss hadn't lasted nearly long enough.

CHAPTER ELEVEN

KERR TOUCHED MY ELBOW TO GAIN MY ATTENTION, AND MY mental fog parted enough to let reality settle in.

"Come, Mya," he said.

He directed me forward, closer to the center of the area where the men would fight. Other fey filtered into the area, too, forming a circle. The majority of them had witnessed what had happened at the feast. Thinking of the angry stares I'd received while horking down those two rolls, I moved closer to Kerr.

The two challenging fey joined Drav on the packed dirt. Their darker skin stood out in comparison to Drav's, and their rage-filled eyes glowed with brighter yellow tints.

Most of the crowd's attention stayed focused on Drav and the two men as they faced off. Some cast glances at me, though, and I could see the burning resentment there. I cringed, wishing I could take back my actions.

A fey stepped up next to me, blocking out most of the irritated glances.

"Mya," Shax said in greeting.

"Hey, Shax. How's the arm?"

He lifted it to show me an almost healed bite.

"Looks good."

The smack of flesh against flesh drew my attention back to the challenge in time to see Drav hop away from Grio. The man stumbled backwards, clutching his bloody, broken nose. Limar snarled and lunged at Drav. Drav swung but missed, enabling Limar to knock him off his feet. As they fell, Drav twisted so they landed on their sides, instead of allowing Limar on top. A plume of black dust rose around them.

While that kind of impact would have knocked the wind from me, neither man seemed to notice. They rolled on the ground, both fighting for control over the other. Meanwhile, Grio shook his head and blew the blood from his nose. With an angry shout, he rushed the pair at the same moment Limar managed to muscle his way to the top.

Drav roared, flexed his arms and kicked up with his legs, using leverage and Limar's weight against him. He flipped the man up and over his head and shoulders. Limar flew into Grio and both men fell hard. Limar's back hit the ground first with a slap, and I flinched as more dust was kicked up.

Limar leapt to his feet and charged Drav. Grio gained his feet, too, but was slower to rejoin the fight. He stood back, studying the pair, and I caught the brief moment Limar's eyes met Grio's.

Drav ducked under Limar's next swing, and Limar

jumped back a step, circling Drav. I saw right away what they were doing. Limar was positioning Drav so he wouldn't see Grio coming. I opened my mouth to call out a warning, but Grio moved too fast.

He rushed forward and had Drav's head in his hands.

"Drav!" I shouted in panic.

I took a step forward. Kerr moved in front of me, protecting me from myself, but also blocking the fight from my view.

"I'm good. I promise," I said hurriedly.

Shaking, I leaned around him, dreading what I'd see.

Grio sat on the ground, holding his nose once more. Limar threw his arms out to catch Drav around the waist, but Drav ducked and landed a strong fist into the man's gut. Limar grunted and backed away, doubled over.

Heart in my throat, I watched in relief, knowing Drav had narrowly avoided a very dangerous situation. Drav spared me a glance before his attention returned to the two men he fought.

"Why is this necessary? All because I ate before someone?"

Kerr grunted, but it was Shax who answered. Most of it I couldn't understand, but I caught Phusty's name intermingled with the other words. I had no idea what that might signify. The men were more upset about what had happened to Phusty?

A loud roar echoed around us as Drav trapped Limar in a headlock. Grio jumped to his feet and pounded on Drav's back and softer sides. The brutal thuds reverberated around the otherwise silent circle. Pain flickered on Drav's face, but the muscles in his arm tightened around the neck in his grasp.

My lungs emptied of air, and my attempt to inhale caught in my throat.

Drav wrapped his hand in Limar's hair and, with a mighty cry, pulled back. His muscles bulged as he tore Limar's head from his shoulders.

Blood splattered on the ground. Even though I should have been prepared since I'd witnessed Drav do it before, this time was so different. This time, the fight really had been my fault. All because of two stupid cabbage rolls. I sniffled slightly. Shax glanced at me, but I didn't turn away from the scene of death before me.

The coppery tang of blood filled the air, and my stomach churned. Drav, Ghua, and the others had made such a big deal out of Phusty's death. And, two criminals had been exiled for the death of another fey. If death upset them so much, why were the challenges centered around killing each other?

Drav tossed Limar's head aside, and no one in the surrounding group even blinked an eye. I seemed to be the only one upset by the ordeal. Grio didn't seem particularly angry that his partner was gone.

Covered in Limar's blood, Drav faced off with Grio.

As much as I needed Drav to win, my focus didn't stray from Limar's remains. The blood stopped gushing from the stump of his neck, and his arms and legs twitched. I waited for a sign that he would heal like the animals in the vision, that his head would grow back or reattach or something.

Instead, the body vanished, leaving behind a flat pair of pants.

My mouth dropped open.

"Wh-what?"

I glanced at Drav, who circled Grio. Blood dripped from Drav's nose now, too, and his breaths were labored. Grio was in much worse shape with a fat lip and a cut above his eye. He breathed even harder than Drav.

It didn't matter. Seeing Drav hurt and bleeding spiked my anger. This whole challenge was ridiculous. No one should die over the fact that I took a bite of food first. Or because Phusty had attacked Drav first, to get to me. Drav was only trying to protect me.

I stepped forward ready to try to stop this from going any further, but Kerr grabbed my arm. His grasp, not unlike Drav's when we first met, bit into my skin. I cried out in surprise. Kerr obviously didn't realize his strength.

A familiar roar reached my ears, and I looked over to find Drav glaring at Kerr. The rage painting his features worried me, and I swatted Kerr's hand to get him to release me. He did, but not soon enough based on Drav's murderous gaze.

Grio took the distraction as an opportunity to attack Drav again and lunged forward, grabbing the back of Drav's head. He fisted Drav's hair around his hand and yanked backwards.

The move only pissed off Drav more. He reached back and grabbed the hand tangled in his hair. Snarling, he bent forward, throwing Grio over his shoulder.

Grio landed hard in front of Drav, his head slamming against the ground. None of the men jeered or heckled the fallen man. They remained quiet, watching the fight with rapt attention as Drav kneeled on Grio's chest and pummeled his face. Blood spurted from Grio's nose, splattering Drav's already blood soaked chest.

"Drav!"

His face twisted in rage as he continued to pound on Grio. I called his name one more time before he finally stopped. Grio's face was a bloody mess, and the man didn't move. I wasn't even sure he still breathed.

Certain that Drav would get up now, I wasn't prepared when he reached down, grabbed the sides of Grio's head, and tore it away with a gag-inducing sound.

I stepped back as Drav threw the head away and it rolled to the other side of the circle. The fey, who had gathered to watch, nodded in Drav's direction and began to disburse.

Drav turned toward us. His tangled braids were shiny with blood, and it looked like a darkening bruise colored his chest. Blood dripped down his face and from his knuckles. I wasn't sure how badly he was hurt and hesitated to step forward to find out.

Drav still looked ready to kill someone. But he wasn't looking at me.

Kerr stepped back, looking ashamed. Shax stayed by my side as Drav made his way over.

"Thank you, Shax," Drav said. Shax nodded then left with the rest.

Drav bypassed me and stepped up to Kerr, speaking in their language, his voice harsh. My name was thrown in there, and I stepped forward with the intention of halting

Drav from whatever he might do. Yet again, I was too slow. Drav drew back and landed a punch to Kerr's right eye. Kerr didn't seem upset about the attack as he faced me.

"Ego veniam," Kerr said, bending at the waist in a sweeping bow.

Confused and annoyed by the whole shit storm I'd just witnessed, I shook my head and glared at Drav.

"What the hell is going on?"

"Kerr apologized."

Kerr took that as his cue to leave and stepped around us.

"You didn't have to punch him. He didn't mean to hurt me."

"But he did hurt you."

I rubbed my face, trying to stay calm.

"He stopped me from interfering, Drav. A mild grip on my arm. Nothing compared to what you just did. You killed those men!"

"Yes, to protect you. They will not bother you any longer."

"Yeah, no kidding. Dead people usually don't bother anyone. And what the hell happened to their bodies?"

"The crystals protected them."

"No, I'm pretty sure they didn't. You ripped off their heads, just like you did to everyone who annoyed you on the surface. I very much doubt their crystals can heal that."

Drav looked frustrated, and threaded his bloody fingers through mine. He tugged me forward in the direction of the waterfall. I tried to pull away, unsure that I wanted to go anywhere with him just then. I was relieved that he was safe, but I needed a minute to process what the hell had just happened.

"Come." Drav pulled me more insistently. I glanced at his gory chest and knew I needed to keep up or risk being carried.

The sounds from the river, the quiet babble of water and the occasional random splash, grew louder as we neared.

"Drav..."

"I will show you, Mya."

At the river, some of the men from the challenge gathered near an inlet. They stared at the still waters pooled there. I looked, too. Two completely bare-assed men were emerging from the depths. I quickly spun around.

"Mya, look," Drav said, gently tugging my fingers.

Did he seriously want me to eye up two naked men?

"What is the point of this, Drav?" I asked, feeling the heat in my cheeks.

"Do you not recognize them?"

"What are you talking about?"

"Turn around and look."

Huffing a breath, I did as he asked but kept my eyes trained on the men's faces. They met my gaze. Both nodded respectfully at me and repeated the same words Kerr had used before leaving us. Why were these guys apologizing to me?

It took another moment for me to recognize them. Grio and Limar stood in the thigh deep waters, both completely bald. No hair on their heads, eyebrows or...

I quickly shifted my gaze to Drav.

"Why are they bald now?"

"We come back hairless."

"Come back. How...how is that possible?" In the vision, everything they had killed had healed, not disappeared.

"The crystal protects us."

Not just protection, and far more than resurrection. All those times he'd ripped off the heads on the surface had he thought his victims would come back like this? Was that why it had been so easy for him to kill?

I stared at Drav, unsure how to react.

"All the heads you took off up on the surface...did you think they would come back?"

"Yes."

My eyes started to burn with unshed tears. As much as I'd started to like him, another part of me had held onto the fact he'd coldly killed so many. But that wasn't who he was.

Concern etched his features when he saw my tears, and he stepped closer. I stopped him before he could set his forehead to mine. He was still covered in blood. Some of which belonged to him.

"You need to clean up," I said. "And when you're done, you have my permission."

A wide grin split his lips.

"Yes." The drawn out, triumphant way he said it set my heart racing.

CHAPTER TWELVE

DRAV TOOK MY HAND AND LED ME FURTHER UP THE RIVER where the waterfall crashed down. Other men swam in the churning waters. I waited for Drav to dive in and join them, but he didn't. He turned to me with an intense look in his eyes.

The roar of the water filled my ears until he leaned in and said four little words that sent a bolt of panic and desire through me.

"Take your clothes off."

I jerked back and looked into his eyes to see if he was serious. Raw determination lit his gaze, and he reached down to tug at the tie holding up his pants. My gaze followed, and my mouth went dry when the material pooled around his ankles. Completely unashamed of his nudity, he stood still and let me stare at his massive erection. My face heated, but for the life of me, I couldn't bring myself to look away for several long seconds.

When I finally did, he kicked his pants aside with an indifference that didn't match the stark hunger in his eyes. He reached out, this time to tug at the hem of my shirt.

"Why?" I managed to croak.

He trailed his fingers along the side of my neck.

"So I can look at you and touch your softness."

I shivered and swallowed hard, wanting that too, more than I thought possible.

Someone moved in the water behind him, reminding me that we had an audience. I stepped back, and he shadowed me, denying me the distance I needed to think clearly.

"W-what about everyone else? I don't want them watching and getting ideas."

Drav turned his head, glancing on the few men washing in the water, then at the men who had followed us.

"Go. Mya wants to bathe in private."

"What?" I squeaked.

Drav's gaze pinned me as the men left the water. I tried again to put some space between us, but he followed me, step for step, until he reached out and gripped my waist and pulled flush to his torso. Anchored against him, I felt his desire. He lifted my hand and placed it around his neck. Heart beating rapidly, I held still as he lowered his head and tenderly kissed my bottom lip. Just that small contact made my knees weaken and reminded me of the kiss before the fight. I wanted that again. Badly.

Just enough sanity remained to discourage the idea. If I fully gave in to him, would he ever take me home? But he wasn't asking for everything. Just a kiss...

Drav's heat radiated from his bare skin, warming me. Enticing me to lift my lips more fully to his.

Someone called out a few words and laughed. I turned my head away and saw the retreating backs of several bare-assed men.

"Bathe with me, Mya," Drav said against my ear. "I will teach you what plants to use for washing."

I exhaled shakily.

"If it's all right with you, I'd rather just sit here and wait until you're done." My voice shook as I spoke, a sign of how much he tempted the hell out of me.

He pulled back and frowned slightly, but stepped away. The corded muscles of his back and tight ass held my attention as he walked to the water's edge. I tore my gaze from his fluid dive into the pool and saw all the men had left us. No one even lingered at the distant tournament grounds. No witnesses if I really did want to bathe. No witnesses but Drav.

Indecision had me turning back to the water. As if anticipating my uncertainty, I found him watching me from where he swam in the middle of the pool.

"Last time I got near some water, a fish tried to eat my face," I said loud enough for him to hear.

"There are no fish in these waters. I will keep you safe."

I shook my head and sat on the edge. A few sure strokes brought him close to me.

"Are you afraid of the water?" he asked.

"No. I can swim and normal fish don't really bother me."

"Are you afraid of me?"

"No."

"Then why won't you bathe with me?"

He had me there.

"I don't know. I guess I am afraid. But I'm not sure what I'm afraid of," I said, not wanting to put into words my concern about him keeping me down here forever.

He nodded slightly then swam to the far edge to pluck a few leaves from one of the plants. While he rubbed them between his hands, I considered my hesitation. The thought of cleaning up did appeal to me. I hadn't showered since we'd left the cabin. Undoubtedly, I smelled. And, some of the blood that had coated Drav now clung to my clothes. So why not hop in? It wasn't like I was overly shy. I'd walked around the dorm halls in a t-shirt and underwear for Pete's sake. What was my problem?

I glanced across the pool at the big, grey guy soaping his broad, chiseled chest and knew my problem lay with how much I really didn't want to wear anything if I joined him.

"Screw it," I mumbled, toeing off my shoes. I peeled off my socks, and with a quick glance over my shoulder, I stripped down to my panties. Before he could notice, I jumped into the water.

The chilly temperature hit me like a fist, and I came up gasping and squealing. Drav's warm arms immediately wrapped around me, and I clung to the only source of heat.

"Did you hurt yourself?" he asked, concern clipping his words.

"Yes! This is f-fucking cold!" I attempted to wipe water

from my face as I wrapped my legs around his waist. He held me close and rubbed my back as I shook.

"Why would anyone bathe in this?"

His lips skimmed my neck in a very pleasant way. Yet, as much as he'd interested me outside of the water, the temperature had helped cool that.

"I'm not trying to play hard to get or anything, but if I stay in this water too long, I might end up with hypothermia. Can you show me how to wash so we can get out?"

His immediate alarm assured me he understood. Keeping his hold on me, he swam to the other side then started crushing leaves again. His body heat made the water barely tolerable, so I continued to cling to him while he washed my hair for me. When it came time to rinse, I hesitated, not wanting to submerge again. However, it didn't feel as shocking the second time, which worried me.

Hating to give up my only source of warmth, I moved out of his arms enough to remove my underwear and finished washing in a hurry.

"Drav," a voice called.

I froze and stared at Drav with wide, panicked eyes. The water lapped at my collarbones, covering me. But I couldn't stay in the water much longer. With an arm looped around Drav's neck for support, I turned to look at the opposite bank.

Molev stood there with my shirt pressed to his nose.

"Oh, c-come on," I stuttered. However, I got over my annoyance rather quickly when I saw he held a clean shirt in his other hand.

"I'm d-done," I said to Drav.

He crossed the pool of water with me wrapped around him.

"Mya would like you to turn around. Looking at her without clothes makes her uncomfortable," Drav said before I could.

I pressed a quick kiss to his jaw in appreciation while Molev turned around without complaint. Drav lifted me out of the water and set me on the bank. The warmer air made the shivering worse and without Drav's hand, I wouldn't have been able to stand. His gaze swept over me, and I didn't miss the irony of what he'd just said to Molev. Drav's gaze no longer made me uncomfortable, though. Besides, I looked my fill, too. The water had done nothing to wither his desire for me.

Ignoring his heated expression, I gestured at the clean shirt in Molev's hand.

"Can I wear that?"

The man said something in their language.

"He brought it for you," Drav said.

"Thank you," I said, plucking the shirt from his fingers.

Molev began talking again, his tone conversational, unlike when I'd heard him at the tree.

"Can you tell me what he's saying?" I asked Drav just before I tugged the shirt on over my wet skin. The soft, dry material fell to my knees, giving me enough cover that I tossed my wet underwear to my pile of dirty clothes.

Drav made no move to dress or hide what the water hadn't cooled.

"He heard what happened at the meal and came to

congratulate me," he said, translating. "He also wanted to see you without clothes."

"Not happening," I muttered, gathering up my things.

Molev turned around and waved at the dirty garments while speaking.

"Leave them," Drav said. "Grio and Limar will wash them."

I dropped the pile again. If someone else wanted to wash my stuff, fine by me. I just wanted to get warm.

"Please tell me you have blankets hidden around here somewhere."

"We do," Drav said. "May I carry you back?"

"Please."

He had me up in his arms, but thankfully didn't run. The wind on my wet hair would have made my chill worse. Molev fell into step beside Drav. While they walked, they talked. Mostly Molev asked questions that Drav answered with descriptions of the surface. However, when he said no animals existed above, I had to correct him.

"They exist. They just ran off when the earthquakes happened. I'm not sure where they went. Actually, we did see that normal dog, remember?" I said, looking up at Drav. "And it isn't just my world, it's our world. Yours and mine. The crystal showed me that you had all come from the surface, too. Your own people trapped you down here and took your memories. If you came up to the surface and let my people get to know you, I think you'd like it up there."

Molev grunted but said nothing. At the base of the tree,

he waved us off and I closed my eyes. Tucking my face against Drav, I waited for the breeze to stop.

"We're here, Mya."

I opened my eyes and looked around in surprise. The burl had my bag but looked nothing like it had previously. Numerous crystal lanterns lay scattered about the room, giving everything a pretty, soft glow. And everything included a mound of cloth stacked on the bed.

"What is that?" I asked.

"The material we use to make our clothes. It's all we have that is close to blankets."

"You don't use blankets?"

"No."

Damn.

"Let me know who I need to thank for bringing them here."

"Probably Kerr. While we were traveling, he noticed you became cold easily."

I owed Kerr big time. Without waiting for an invitation, I walked over to the bed and burrowed in under half the pieces, using the bottom half as a cushion. Still shivering, I looked up at Drav and lifted the covers.

"You joining me?"

He smiled and climbed in next to me. His body heat, and his hands gently rubbing my arms, helped warm me. In the soft light, we stared at each other. I wanted him to kiss me again. A lot. And that troubled me.

"I thought you'd be all over me after I gave you permission," I said.

"I want to, but you look sad. I don't want you to take your permission away."

"I won't. I'm just…I don't know where this is going to go," I said. "Not right now, this moment, but in the long run. My people are afraid of you guys now. Of you, the hellhounds, and the infected. People in fear do stupid things. They don't think. And that scares me as much as it scares you. But not enough to hide away forever."

I sighed and snuggled in against his chest.

"I don't want to stay down here," I said, softly. "I want to go back to the surface with you. Both our kinds belong up there. But, what if my people see you and try hurting you again? I don't want you hurt. And I don't want you hurting any of them. We're not like you. When you rip off our heads, that's it. That's the end."

I pulled back and looked into his eyes as I said what was really on my mind.

"That ache you feel? I feel it, too. More each day. And I think that ache is going to cause us both problems."

"We will face any problems together," he said. "I will keep you safe."

He pressed his lips to mine, a gentle kiss, then tucked me more securely against his bare chest.

"Rest, Mya. We will talk more when you wake."

Snuggling close, I closed my eyes and let his warmth lull me. I wasn't quite asleep when he whispered, "Do I still have permission to touch you?"

"Yes," I said softly.

His hand crept under my shirt, and he lay his palm

against my breast. It felt hot compared to my skin and oh so good.

"Thank you for asking."

"Thank you for saying yes."

I WOKE with a headache and groaned. The murmur of masculine voices nearby quieted.

"Are you hungry?" Drav asked.

When I lifted my head, I saw he'd dressed. He and Molev stood on the far side of the room next to my bag.

"No, I'm okay. What's going on?" I asked, feeling oddly exposed. I tugged the covers more securely around my waist as I sat up. It was weird knowing they'd been having a conversation in here while I still slept.

"Molev has suggested that we go to Lacus."

"What's Lacus, and why do we need to go?"

"It is like an ocean but not so big. We don't need to go. He thought you might enjoy seeing it."

"A lake?"

"Yes," Drav said with a smile.

"Where is it?"

"Outside of the city. Only one rest away if I carry you."

Outside of the city meant hellhound lands. But it also meant we would be that much closer to the surface tunnels. With the men being told to return, we might run into some who had news about up top. I hoped the bombings had stopped.

It wasn't only the thought of news that had me considering. A trip anywhere would mean more alone time with Drav. After giving him permission to touch me, I really wanted more time together.

"What would we be doing at this lake?"

"Noodling," Drav said with a smile, making my heart thump just a little harder because he'd remembered.

Molev glanced at Drav with confusion, and I snorted.

"Molev also said that by the time we return from the lake, the rest of the men should be back with information. If we went, you would not be bothered by the new men, and I can teach you how we fish."

I'd already decided it was a good idea, but knowing it would get me away from the sniffing, stares, and attempts to see what lay beneath my clothes sealed the deal.

"It would be just me and you?" I asked, just to be sure.

"Yes."

"Wouldn't that be too dangerous?"

"I will keep you safe, Mya. We will only travel the lit caverns."

I nodded.

"Okay. Well, I need my clothes." I looked at my bag sitting near their feet. Drav picked it up and handed it to me. However, neither of them seemed ready to leave once I had new clothes out. I looked at them expectantly and arched a brow.

Drav grunted.

"Do you wish for us to turn around?"

"Yes."

Molev did without hesitation, but Drav moved a little bit slower. Poor guy. I told him he had permission then made him turn away. I'd need to explain that permission only worked when we were alone.

After changing in record time, I told them it was okay to look again then shouldered my bag.

"Leave that, Mya," Drav said gently. "We need to travel light, and we will find food on the way."

"Oh." It made sense since Drav had to carry me. But, I hesitated to just leave the bag in his doorless hut. I didn't want anything to happen to it while we were away. It had my phone, my life line to contacting Ryan when we got back to the surface.

"Mya?"

"I'm being silly, but will my bag be safe here?" Drav had said stealing was forbidden, but I needed their word.

"Yes, it is safe. No one will use our room."

"Okay." Setting the bag on the bed, I went to him. "Let's go noodling."

CHAPTER THIRTEEN

DRAV RAN TIRELESSLY THROUGH THE LIT CAVERN. INSTEAD OF focusing on my niggling headache, I studied him. The strong line of his jaw. His proud nose. The curve of his lower lip. I couldn't ignore the pulse of desire that shot through me at the thought of having him to myself for the next couple of days. Suppressing a grin, I began to play with the hair at the back of his neck.

He glanced down at me, then my boobs, then back up again. Having fun, I reached a little higher and trailed a finger along the edge of his opposite ear. His speed decreased.

"Don't slow down," I said. "I want to get to our resting spot so we can kiss some more."

Wind lashed at me as he sprinted, and I laughed.

It didn't seem to take too long before he stopped.

"We will rest here," he said firmly.

The bright light of the cavern seemed to make my head

thump a little worse, but I determinedly ignored it as Drav eased me to my feet.

"Was this the place you had in mind or are you improvising because you want a kiss?"

"Improvising." That was the last word he said before his lips claimed mine.

The heat of his kiss burned away thoughts of headaches, bombings, missing family, and hellhounds. Nothing else existed but me and the man whose hands smoothed down the curve of my back to cup my butt. I let him explore, reveling in the feel of his firm touch. All his caresses sent sparks of fire into my already heated blood.

His lips left mine, and he looked down at me.

"Wherever you go, I will follow and keep you safe. Whatever you need, I will provide it for you. I am yours Mya, in every lifetime."

He said the words with such burning intensity, my insides melted further. How could someone so different come to mean so much to me? I didn't know.

"And I'm yours," I said, heart pounding.

I loved the way he kissed me and touched me and knew he felt the same. Yet, everything was so new to him, and he probably had no idea what he liked. Eager to learn more about him, I slipped my hands under his shirt and slid my palms up the flat plains of his stomach. He made a small sound, a mix of exhale and pained groan.

"Do you want me to stop?" I asked.

"No. You have my permission to touch me how you like."

I grinned and slid my hands up further, my fingertips

brushing his flat nipples. They pebbled under my touch, and his fingers twitched on my back. Circling the softer skin, I watched his expression. His gaze grew hungrier, and he claimed my lips for another searing kiss that made my toes curl.

Pushing his shirt up, I waited for him to break the kiss then moved my attention to his broad chest. He slid his hands from my back to my hips, and he gripped me firmly as I pressed my lips against his sternum. The smooth feel of his skin and his racing pulse notched my need for him higher.

He arched into me, pressing the bulge of his erection near my bellybutton. His size brought a moment of worry.

"You won't take more than I'm ready to give, right?"

"I will take nothing you do not give freely."

Reassured, I traced the indent between his pectorals with my tongue. A hiss escaped him when I veered to the right and circled around his nipple.

"You still okay?" I whispered against his skin.

"Yes." The rough word grated with need, his breathing ragged.

"If I do something you don't like, let me know, and I'll stop."

"I like everything you do," he said.

While I kissed my way to the left side, I slid my hands lower to the waist of his pants. His breathing stopped.

"Keep breathing, Drav," I whispered just before I lightly nipped his nipple and grasped his erection.

His groan echoed in the cavern, and he pressed firmly

into my hand. The urgency in which he tipped my head back and kissed me hard, stole my air and fed my hunger.

He arched against me again, a demand and a plea. Wrapping my hand around him, as much as his pants would allow, I firmly stroked him. After thousands of years alone, that single touch undid him. With a cry, he stiffened and held me to him. I could feel him pulsing under my palm.

His fingers threaded through my hair, and he kissed me deeply until I was breathless.

"Magic did not die in your world because you still live," he whispered against my hair.

I HAD NEVER BEEN to the ocean but was familiar with big lakes. Oklahoma had a lot of them. However, the sight before me proved more stunning than anything I'd seen before. No waves or wind disturbed the still surface. Not even a bubble. Small patches of crystals on the vast ceiling above the water and those underneath the surface illuminated the body from both sides, making the liquid a glowing crystal-blue. It appeared unnatural, but beautiful, with the rock formations and vegetation surrounding the lake reflecting back on its surface.

Drav led us into the surrounding trees, much smaller than those in their city but not like the orchard trees, either. These had large grey leaves that draped over a silver trunk with no branches. A brown ivy with tiny leaves grew up the trunks, completely covering the tree. Between the thick vines that dropped down amid the large leaves of the trees, I caught glimpses of round, yellow globes that looked like some type of fruit.

As pretty as everything was, I had a hard time staying focused on our surroundings instead of Drav's firm ass ahead of me. After his happy ending during our explosive little make out session, I'd insisted we rest like we were supposed to. However, I had actually fallen asleep instead of just giving him enough time to recoup. When I'd woken, it had been to him already carrying me to our final destination. I'd decided to play it cool and wait, but after hours of fantasizing what we might end up doing once we'd reached the lake, I'd had to ask to walk when I'd caught myself eyeing his chorded neck.

Now, I was only waiting for him to point out where we were bedding down for our stay.

Drav stopped walking, and my hope surged until he pulled some of the fallen ivy from the ground.

"What is the word for this?" he asked.

"Looks kinda like ivy to me."

"We need to collect some for the fish."

I wrinkled my nose but pitched in to gather what he needed. When Drav declared that we had enough, we moved closer to the lake's edge where he sat down and indicated for me to join him.

"So what are we doing?"

"We will build a net."

Drav stuck two thick sticks in the ground before us. Then, he reached into a small pouch from his belt and pulled out a wooden tool pointed on one end with a small shaped hole near the top. He set it next to me and pulled out a second one.

"We will use the tools to make nets. Here."

Drav grabbed the ivy and began to wrap it around the tool he had set next to me. After watching him for a bit, I picked it up and followed suit. Once they were wrapped, Drav demonstrated what to do next. It was a lot of the same work over and over. While he labored with a practiced ease and patience, I grew bored and kept thinking back to our prior rest.

I grinned slightly.

"You are happy?" he asked.

"Mostly. I was thinking of last night."

His lips curved.

"We will finish the net, feed you, and kiss some more."

His hands flew through the weaving pattern he'd attempted to show me. Once he had a completed net, he stood, handed it to me, then pulled the string to his pants.

"Not that I'm complaining, but what are you doing?"

"We will be going into the water. It will take a long time for our clothes to dry if we do not remove them." He punctuated that statement by dropping his pants and tugging his shirt over his head.

Drav held out his hand for the net, but I couldn't take my eyes off him.

"Come, Mya. We must fish."

"Right." I tore my gaze from his impressive length and handed over the net.

Drav walked to the edge of the water and waded in. He

stopped once the water reached his waist and looked back at me expectantly.

Flushing, I pulled off my shirt and unbuttoned my jeans. Drav watched with rapt interest as I slid them down my legs. When I reached behind my back, he turned in the water so he fully faced me. The tender way his gaze swept over me from head to foot eased some of my nerves. I unclasped my bra and shrugged it off my shoulders.

"You are beautiful, Mya," he said with awe.

"Thank you. You are too." With my underwear still on, I stepped toward the edge.

"You should take that off or it will get wet."

"I'll risk it."

His lips twitched.

"Don't laugh. I don't trust what's in that water."

"Nothing will harm you. Come." He held his hand out, waiting for me to join him.

The water was warmer than the river, but it still wasn't like climbing into a relaxing hot tub. I took Drav's hand when I reached him, and I was glad I did because I slipped on a rock and stumbled forward, right into his chest. Without his hold, I would have landed face first in the water.

"Oof, sorry," I said, balancing myself against him. He held my hand steadily and allowed me to use his chest to right myself.

"Are you okay, my Mya?"

"Yeah, I'm good." I saw some strands of Drav's hair had come out of his braids and brushed away the ones that had dropped over his forehead.

"We must stay very still. We will scare the fish."

"I sincerely hope these are not the same fish I encountered when we first arrived."

"No, you are safe."

I began to ease backwards but Drav tightened his arm around my waist and kept me close.

"We cannot move."

Water lapped at my bellybutton.

"How will we catch fish then?" I whispered.

"Don't worry, I will catch us dinner."

"I don't like raw fish."

"You need to eat."

"There was fruit in the trees."

"Shh..." he said softly, his gaze shifting to the right.

I stiffened as I glanced over. A small school of fish swam closer to us. More specifically, our toes. Drav released his hold around my waist and moved in a blink of an eye.

The water splashed around us, spraying me. When I opened my eyes, I found Drav holding the net out proudly. Inside thrashed several dripping wet see-through fish.

"That's amazing, Drav!"

I leaned forward, in awe of their translucent bodies, and slipped slightly again. I caught myself on his chest, but in the process, my breast brushed his arm. My nipple pebbled at the contact, and I shivered. He growled, dropped the fish net, and held me to his chest.

His intense gaze captured mine as he reached up and stroked a finger over my hard nipple. A small gasp escaped me. Warm heat spread from his fingertip down to my belly.

His focus shifted to my parted lips as he continued to tease my breast.

"So soft," he said a moment before he dipped his head and brushed his lips against mine.

Another shiver ripped through me, spreading the heat further south. He inhaled against my skin and deepened the kiss, his tongue seeking entrance. I opened and dissolved into his embrace. His mouth and fingers made everything disappear except for the growing need burning inside me.

Something jumped in the water beside us, a reminder of our location. I pulled away to breathe, and Drav pressed his forehead against mine.

"You dropped the fish," I said.

"It was worth it."

"We don't have dinner now."

"There is fruit in the trees."

I laughed and pressed another quick kiss on his firm lips.

When we finished the fruit he'd quickly collected, Drav made us a bed from the large fronds. He lay down naked and stretched out on his back, his erection proudly exposed. Moisture still glistened on his skin. Between the dip in the lake and the humidity in the air, he'd been right. It would have taken a long time for my clothes to dry. As it was, my wet underwear still clung to me uncomfortably.

"Are we really safe in here?"

"Yes. The blue and green crystals both exist here so there is never darkness. No hounds will enter here."

Taking a steadying breath, I hooked my fingers in my underwear and pulled them off to hang them over a nearby frond. When I turned around, Drav observed me with an intensity that made me nervous.

Neither of us moved for several long minutes.

"I won't touch you if you've changed your mind," he said, softly.

"I haven't changed my mind. I'm just crazy nervous."

He sat up and held out his hand.

"If I do something you don't like, let me know, and I'll stop."

An ache grew in my chest at hearing those words. Taking his hands, I stepped closer. His gaze dropped to the patch of hair that had so fascinated him at the cabin then back up to my face.

"Will you snuggle with me, Mya?"

I nodded and lay down beside him.

His fingers skimmed over my skin from belly to breast as he leaned over to kiss me. His tongue teased mine until I forgot to be nervous and panted for air. When his mouth left mine and his kisses trailed down the column of my throat, I turned my head to give him better access. The entire time, his fingers never stopped moving. They drifted over my navel, then lower. I grinned slightly, knowing his curiosity was killing him.

His lips closed over my nipple, obliterating humor with a burning need between my legs. I curled my fingers in his hair. His lips moved to my other breast, and his teeth gently nipped me as his fingers slid over my folds.

Panting, I opened for him. Conscious thought fled as his lips trailed lower. His breath fanned against my bellybutton before going further south. My gasp echoed in the cave when he kissed the sweet spot between my legs. I involuntarily bucked under him.

"Do you want me to stop?" he asked, pulling back.

"Please don't," I panted.

He kept going, his tongue teasing and stroking every inch of me until I pulsed and cried out in a long, low wail.

Limp and relaxed, I twitched under Drav's lips as he kissed his way back up to my breast, where he set his head.

"That is how my heart raced after you touched me," he said softly. "Sleep, Mya. When you wake, we will snuggle some more."

With him half draped over me, I closed my eyes and reveled in the feel of his light touch as I drifted off to sleep.

In the morning, Drav lay beside me, a piece of fruit in his hand.

"Thank you," I said, sitting up with a wince. The headache from the day before had only grown worse. Not wanting it to wreck our remaining time, I brushed away his concern and let him show me how to peel and eat the fruit. As I nibbled, so did he. But not on the fruit. It was, by far, the best meal I'd ever had and helped distract me from the thumping behind my eyes.

The relief didn't last beyond the final fading tremor, though.

"I'm not feeling really good. I wish I would have brought my bag," I said, thinking of the pain reliever I had in the first aid kit.

"Dress. We can go back."

"You don't want to snuggle more?"

"Not when you don't feel well," he said with a kiss to my temple.

I was mildly disappointed then reminded myself the sooner we returned, the sooner we could head back to the surface for some privacy with a real bed.

He packed up the tools he had brought with him but left the fish net. Without needing to ask, he lifted me and took off toward the city.

The motion didn't help. Not only did the pain in my head grow worse, but my stomach started to roll. When he stopped for the resting period I didn't sleep as soundly. My stomach cramped continually, and I moved restlessly. Drav worried the whole time. Obviously, the fruit we had eaten wasn't sitting well. As soon as the cave's crystals dimmed, we started toward the city, and I tried to ignore the increasing pain in my stomach.

Hours later, the wall appeared, and the door opened well before we reached it. Drav went right through.

"Do you want to walk for a bit?" Drav asked, concern in his tone.

"Yeah. Maybe it'll help my stomach."

It didn't. I changed my mind about the illness stemming from weird fruit to possible period cramps. I couldn't remember how many days it had been. Too much had happened.

Drav laced his fingers between mine, and we walked to the city. It definitely buzzed with more activity and men who stared at me with curiosity.

Drav picked me up when we arrived at our tree, and he ran up the steps to our burl. The relief I felt at the welcome sight of our home died when Drav entered.

Molev sat on the bed. The white cords of the iPod's earbuds stood out starkly against his black shirt. He stared down in rapt interest at the glowing iPod cradled in his large hand.

"Put me down," I said to Drav, pissed.

Molev noticed us and stood, tugging the earbuds out of his ears. He nodded in greeting.

"Thank you, Mya. Your language is very interesting to learn."

CHAPTER FOURTEEN

In full blown bitch mode, I marched up to Molev and grabbed the iPod out of his hands. The battery icon blinked in the corner. How long had he been listening? I flipped through the list of previous books and cringed. All romance novels. I wanted to swear.

"You didn't have permission," I said.

"I apologize. I was returning the clothes that Grio and Limar washed and was curious about you and your world and looked at your things. I meant no harm. When I accidently turned this on, my curiosity only grew stronger. I'm glad I found it and learned your language, though. I have many questions for you, Mya."

His calm sincerity and lack of any perverseness defused my anger. However, the pulse of my headache grew more pronounced.

"I'll answer what I can," I said, placing the iPod back in the bag and digging out the first aid kit. The sight of two foil pain reliever packets comforted me. Both men watched as I ripped one of the packets open and downed the pills. Setting the bottle of water aside, I got cozy on the blankets and looked up at Molev.

"What's your first question?"

Drav sat beside me and began to soothingly rub my back and shoulders. I loved him touching me. It was both a reassurance and a comfort. I couldn't seem to get enough of him.

Molev resumed his relaxed position by the entrance and studied us for a moment.

"When you went to the source, it didn't give you a life crystal, but something else. Tell me, what did you see?"

I repeated the story of the history I'd been shown, and how the deer coming back to life started it all. When I finished, Molev nodded slowly.

"We are connected with the magic here. Phusty's death proved that."

"Connected, but should you be? I think the magic here changed you. Your skin. Your eyes. I'm not saying it's bad, just that you've had to adapt to live in a place you maybe weren't meant to live."

"From what Kerr has told me while you were away, the surface does not sound like a better place to be."

"That's because you didn't know it before the earthquakes and the hellhounds and the infected."

"Tell me what it was like before."

I thought of the woods by the cabin and the peaceful sound

of the birds and the wind. Before I could open my mouth to tell him about all the quiet beauty, other thoughts intruded. Pollution. Prejudices. War. Our world did have beauty, but it had a lot of ugly, too. Well, it had beauty. How much remained now?

With my sorrow, the ache in my head consumed my thoughts.

"Can we talk some more later? My head is really hurting."

"Of course. Rest." He stood and moved toward the entrance.

"Can you take some of these lanterns with you? I think the light's making it worse."

Molev nodded, took several, and walked out.

"Can I get you anything, Mya?" Drav asked.

"No. Can you just keep rubbing me until I fall asleep?"

I closed my eyes and let the gentle swipe of his hand lull me into a slumber where I dreamed I lived with Drav in his underground world forever and eventually forgot about my brother and parents.

When I opened my eyes, the complete darkness puzzled me as did the brush of fingers over my bare breast. When the fingers reached the peak, they gently pinched my nipple, explaining the growing ache between my legs.

"Drav?"

"Yes. I am here. Does your head still hurt?" His fingers continued their slow assault.

"No, not really. Why is it so dark in here?"

"The light seemed to bother you, even in your sleep, so I

removed the lanterns and used some of the material to block the rest of the light."

His hand covered my whole breast and gave it a kneading squeeze before moving to the other side. I licked my lips and struggled to focus on my next question.

"Okay. Do I want to know why I'm naked?"

"You undressed."

"I did?" I said, breathlessly. I was brilliant even in my sleep.

"Yes. You threw the clothes across the room, but I don't think you really woke up. I wasn't going to touch you, but you put my hand here."

His fingers circled the circumference of my breast, then skimmed over my pebbled nipple. Unable to help myself, I arched into the touch.

"You've slept a long time."

"And you've been touching me the whole while?"

His fingers stilled.

"Was that wrong?"

"No," I said quickly, not wanting him to stop. "It's okay. I'm just thinking your arm must be tired. I'm sorry I—"

His mouth crashed down on mine, searing me with his unrestrained kiss. My head swam and the tingle of need burned hotter, igniting the aching flesh between my legs. With a groan, I tore my mouth from his. The intention to demand he ditch his clothes, too, died when he kissed his way down to my breast. The heat of his lips and the brush of his tongue tore a gasp from me.

He lifted his head.

"Mya?"

"Don't stop," I panted, grabbing his head and guiding him back. My fingers brushed the long tips of his ears. He groaned and kissed his way to my other breast.

"Drav," a voice called just before dim light flooded the room.

"Shit." I grabbed the nearest bit of cloth, which turned out to be Drav's shirt. Not caring, I yanked him over me for cover.

"Are you fucking?" Molev asked in a calm, curious tone.

"Oh, come on!" I buried my face in Drav's shoulder, appreciating the irony of my current wish to disappear in a deep, dark hole.

"That is not what this is." My words were muffled.

"Then what were you doing? Were those your breasts? What do they taste like, Drav?"

"Kill me now," I mumbled.

Drav growled fiercely and tensed over me.

"No one will kill you."

"Not literally," I said.

He relaxed slightly.

"What do you need, Molev?"

"Solin has just returned. More are on their way from the old orchard hole. Fyllo came back while you slept and said the rest of his group has passed through the gap near the black lake. I would like you both to be there when everyone arrives."

"We will," Drav said.

The light left the room. Neither Drav nor I moved.

"No one will kill you," he repeated with quiet ferocity.

"That's not what I meant. I was just embarrassed he'd seen us making out."

Drav shifted slightly, his weight settling a bit more firmly between my legs. His lips skimmed mine.

"I would like to do more."

"I bet you would, but one interruption is enough. I'd like to get dressed and go figure out when we get to leave."

With a sigh, he rolled off me. Before I could find a replacement cover, light flared in the room. I turned my head and saw Drav standing just inside the entrance, holding a lantern. His wistful gaze swept over me, and I could feel myself start to blush. I sat up and crossed an arm over my breasts.

"Can you turn around? I can't get dress with you watching."

"I don't understand why that makes you uncomfortable. I watched you at the lake."

The lake where we'd been the only two people. Not a tree crawling with men who didn't know how to knock.

"The way you move and the pretty paleness of your skin is so pleasing to me. I would watch you for hours if you let me."

Drav studied me with such intensity that it reminded me of when we first met. Before I was terrified of his reptilian eyes but now I felt pretty, wanted. The raw desire in his expression had me throwing aside my caution, dropping the blanket, and standing. He didn't move from his position near the door as I picked up my underwear. He did, however, make a slight noise when I stepped into them.

His focus never wavered as I dressed piece by piece, in a slow show that would have felt embarrassing with anyone else. The complete fascination in his gaze had me doing things I didn't normally do to get dressed...like smoothing my hands over my breasts and down my sides.

By the time I finished, he looked pained, probably due to the massive erection tenting his pants. He crossed the room and pulled me close.

"When we return, will you take your clothes off again?" he asked, kissing my temple then nuzzling the place below my ear.

"I'll think about it," I said with a small grin, already knowing I would.

I craved his attention more than I cared to acknowledge.

Drav carried me down to the communal table where many men had already gathered. I'd thought there'd been a lot of them before. Their numbers had easily doubled. Men crowded into the lantern strewn clearing, the throng of muscular bodies filling the stump area and spilling over into the surrounding undergrowth.

"Is this everyone?" I asked softly.

"This is more than half, but not all."

Nearby men noticed our arrival and conversation slowly quieted, drawing the attention of Molev, who stood near the communal table. He started our way, his eyes never leaving me.

"If he mentions what he saw, I'm punching him," I said under my breath. Drav grunted.

"Hello, Mya," Molev said when he reached us. "Thank you for joining us. Come. We will eat while we wait."

Relieved, I followed him through the crowd to the three empty stumps near the center. He motioned for me to sit. He and Drav took seats on either side of me. A bald man approached with a leaf stacked with cabbage rolls. He held out the leaf to me first.

"Oh, I'm not falling for this again. Last time I helped myself, people got hurt."

"That won't happen again," Molev assured me. "Eat."

I glanced at Drav, who nodded, before helping myself to two rolls.

"Thanks," I said to the man.

"You're welcome." He turned and offered the rolls to Molev then Drav.

"Thank you, Limar," Molev said.

I did a double take at the man as he walked away.

"Is he being punished? Is that why he's serving dinner?"

"The lowest serve and train until they prove themselves worthy of more," Molev said. "It is not punishment, but protection for them and us."

As I munched, other men brought food to the communal table. Once offerings heaped the surface, Molev stood and turned to me.

"There is more to eat. Come choose," he said.

Drav nudged me until I stood and picked a few things from the table. Molev grabbed some food, then Drav. One by one, the men approached, and I began to notice a slow change in their general appearance. By the time the last bald man helped himself from the picked over remains, I understood the length of their hair related to their social standing. Drav's reaction when I'd put my hair up back home took on a whole different meaning.

A commotion near the far side of the clearing drew my attention. The men stood aside, making it possible to see the new arrivals, who stood out starkly from the rest. Dust coated their grey skin and dark hair, and several of the men had rips or scorch marks on their clothes.

With a weary droop to their shoulders, the travel worn group progressed to the center of the circle where they hungrily helped themselves to what remained of the food. I felt a surge of pity for them and what they'd likely endured on the surface. It conflicted with my impatience to hear the news they brought so we could be on our own way.

A few of the new arrivals noticed me and stared, catching the attention of the rest.

"Tell us what you learned," Molev said, without addressing their curiosity.

Since only Drav and Molev spoke English, I sat between the two of them and listened to the gibberish pouring out of each speaker's mouth. Sometimes, Drav would translate or Molev would ask a question in English so I would get an idea of what was being said.

The men had come from the old orchard and told stories of unintelligent beings who craved flesh and of birds whose shit destroyed anything in a flood of flames. That description of planes, by far, won as my favorite. The men produced different items, explaining their purposes. One man showed a broken cell phone that he said used to glow. Another showed a lighter, which he'd actually figured out how to operate. My amusement ended, though, with the guy who dumped a bag full of canned food on the feast table.

He picked one up and squeezed it, popping the top right off and causing a mass of brown to come squishing out. He brought a finger full to his mouth and, after eating it, explained that he had seen some intelligent beings above who didn't crave flesh. They had eaten what the cans provided.

Drav stood and took one of the cans, which he brought to me.

"Eat," he said.

I looked down at the can of dog food I held, a feeling of devastation overwhelming me. While I safely hid underground, people were up there struggling to survive.

"What happened to the people? The ones eating this?" I asked in a tight voice.

Drav translated the man's answer.

"He killed them and took the cans."

My silent tears fell onto the label.

"I'm sorry, Mya," Drav said softly.

"Tell them what happens when our heads are ripped off. Tell them we don't resurrect from the dead. Tell them they are taking away our lives forever."

Getting angry, I looked up and glared at everyone.

"Those unintelligent people were once like me. But when the hounds came to the surface and started attacking, people got sick. Those uninfected, healthy people you killed were scared and just trying to survive, and you killed them so you can bring fucking dog food down here for show and tell." I threw the can, almost hitting one of the bystanders. It didn't appease my anger.

"I thought this was about sharing real news. All of this is a waste of time. You want real news that won't be at the expense of some innocent person's life? We're just as fucking important as you are. You had no right."

Tears tried to clog my throat.

"No right to kill them, and no right to keep me down here where I'm no help to anyone."

The tears won.

CHAPTER FIFTEEN

DRAV TURNED ME INTO HIS COMFORTING ARMS. HIS HOLD soothed my tears, but not my anger or the increasingly painful thump in my head.

The rational part of me understood Drav, too, had killed humans. That none of these men had known better because they'd lived thousands of years in a place where death did not exist. And, although I understood all of that, I couldn't forget or just "get over" what had been done.

When the tears slowed, I pulled back from Drav and looked at Molev.

"Your people were trapped down here. You had no choice in that. Now, you do have a choice. You know the earthquakes set the hellhounds free on us. Your men have seen what they do to humans...how unprepared we are. Stop hiding underground. Go to the surface and fix the mess you made. And, it is your mess. You ate the cursed deer, which created the hellhounds. Whether accidental or not, the hellhounds exist because of you. Help my people, like yours should have been helped so long ago."

I turned to Drav who'd held me through my speech. The soft lantern light played on his concerned gaze and made my head ache worse. Crying hadn't helped, either.

"Please, can we leave now?" I asked. I desperately wanted to get back to the surface and start the search for my family. Drav bent, as if to pick me up.

"No, you will stay," Molev said. His gaze swept over my tear-stained face.

I opened my mouth to tell him to stick it—Drav and I were going back no matter what—when he cut me off.

"Please. I need you here to help clarify what these men are sharing. Your world is vastly different than ours," he said.

So he wasn't trying to keep me in his world, just at this meeting. I sighed, about to agree, when a jolt of stabbing pain shot right into my head. I hissed a sharp breath and pressed my fingers to my temples, trying to sooth the ache. It didn't help. Instead, a wave of nausea twisted in my stomach. I closed my eyes, hoping it would all fade away, but it didn't. The cramping grew worse.

Perhaps leaving would need to wait for a few hours so I could lay down and rest first.

Drav touched my arm.

"Mya?"

At the anxious concern in his voice, I forced myself to open my eyes and drop my hand to my side. Drav didn't look reassured.

"I'll be fine. Let's hurry up and get this done."

As much as I hated hearing about my people dying unnecessarily, I needed to learn everything I could about the state of the world above before we left.

"We will continue," Molev said after I sat.

The men seemed a little more cautious when they approached us. Some watched me warily as if making sure I didn't have anything nearby to throw at them. Their garbled language became background noise that I began to ignore.

"Mya…" Drav said.

"Hmm?"

"Sain said there was a weapon the intelligent ones were using that made a lot of noise, and something went into his chest and stomach. It took him until he arrived here to heal."

The man in question pointed to the two bloody holes in what remained of his shirt.

"You were shot," I said, amazed that he was still standing. "The humans were using guns to protect themselves."

I felt a stirring of pride toward the other human survivors out there. They weren't helpless, even if these guys could heal quicker or weren't the real threat. As I thought it, another man stepped forward.

The dark fey wasn't dirtied like the rest, and his hair looked a little wet still. He spoke a stream of words which didn't quite sound like their language. It had a familiar ring, but I couldn't place it.

"Fyllo says there were no birds with explosive shit on the surface where he explored," Drav said. "The skies remained clear and the cities whole and quiet."

I frowned, not understanding where he was going with this.

"No bombs?" I asked. That sounded promising. "What did he mean when he said where he explored?"

"The other hole that opened," Drav clarified.

Fyllo took a step forward and hesitantly produced a can of food. He didn't pop it open but handed it to me whole.

He spoke as I looked at the can, and Drav translated.

"He said he found it on the shelf of a building full of food."

I took the can from him realizing he was implying he did not kill anyone for it. I turned the can over, half expecting it to be dog food. Instead, I saw an unfamiliar label with a bright blue background and a plate of sausages on a table. It read, "4 Munchner WeiBwurste." The words he spoke, and the words on the label, clicked into place. German. Of course. They'd suffered quakes, too. My stomach sank a little at the realization it wasn't just our continent that had been affected.

"That other hole leads to Germany? What's happening over there?" For a moment, my headache took a backseat to my curiosity. "Are there any safe places? Did you see any normal humans? Not the infected kind?"

"Yes. Humans," Fyllo said.

"You saw humans?"

Fyllo looked worried, and his gaze darted to Molev then Drav before he spoke again. Drav set his hand on my leg and squeezed it reassuringly. I doubted I would like hearing the translation.

"He said there were many people, most of them infected. He did find a group of humans travelling together, though. He followed them for some time until they arrived at a human stronghold."

Had the Europeans fared better than us? If they weren't dropping bombs there, then perhaps they thought it better to preserve our Earth. Considering we only had one planet, it made more sense to find a solution that didn't involve bombing the hell out of everything.

"What else can you tell me about what's happening over there?"

Fyllo spoke again, but this time, Molev translated.

"He said he followed the humans until they arrived to a safe point, but that is where he got his injury and the news to return."

"Did you notice anything else?" I asked, swallowing hard against my roiling stomach. "Were any of the humans gathering to go look for others? Any military movement to suppress the infected without the use of bombs? Any hope at all that they have a chance of killing the hellhounds on their own?"

"No," Fyllo said clearly.

Drav moved his hand so he was rubbing my back, and it helped ease some of my tension. It didn't matter. I didn't listen to more after that. My mind dwelled on the wasted time since Drav drug me down here. Drav and I could have been up there searching and helping anyone we found. But what could two people do against the mess on the surface? The struggle wasn't just mine or Drav's. It concerned Drav's people, too. They needed to see that. Living down here wasn't living. It was existing.

When the last man finished showing what he'd brought, the rest drifted to speak in smaller groups. Loud chatter came from most of them, along with a few bursts of boisterous laughter here and there. Most likely due to some retelling of tales of their time above ground. Were they laughing at the weak humans? At their struggle to survive when the shadow men could so easily outrun hellhounds and rip off the heads of infected?

Drav rubbed my neck gently, and I realized my hands were clenched into fists.

"Molev, you need to return to the surface. Now. Today. It's where you belong."

"No, down here is safer. We do not have a final death like your people on the surface."

"Safer, but is it better? Do you really want to spend your lives down here like you have been? Now that you've seen the surface and females like me? This isn't where you belong."

"This is where we have lived for thousands of years. This is our home. For now, we will stay. We will revisit this conversation when the birds that shit bombs are gone, and the hounds are far from the crater."

I opened my mouth to argue more when my head blossomed with a pain that would have knocked me off my feet if I had been standing. Black dots clouded my vision. I closed my eyes and gripped my head between my hands.

"Mya?"

Drav's quiet voice sounded like thunder. Bile pooled under my tongue, and I slowly shook my head.

"Home." It was the only word I could manage.

"Yes," Drav said before Molev could get a word in.

A strong set of arms scooped me up. Cradled against a familiar chest, I turned my face into the wind, seeking any sensation to distract from the pain threatening to explode my skull. Within seconds, some of the pain eased. I exhaled slowly and tried to relax as Drav ran, hoping the rest would go away too. The majority of the pain stubbornly remained.

The sensation of Drav racing up the tree stopped along with the wind. His growl had me opening my eyes. Men crowded the branch which held our burl. Some moved to and from other burls further out, others lounged outside the burls, talking to one another.

At our appearance, someone called out Drav's name and everyone's attention turned to us.

Drav didn't put me down but moved right for the entrance of our temporary home. No material covered the opening like before. The pile of "blankets" no longer waited inside on the wooden bed either.

Drav growled again.

"Where did everything go?" I asked. I wanted to block out the weak crystal light, burrow under the blankets, and fall asleep until my head stopped hurting and I didn't feel like hurling my rolls.

A voice come from behind Drav, who grunted then translated.

"They needed to replace damaged clothing." He turned. "Can you hand Mya the bag?"

The man standing nearby picked up the bag and handed it over.

"Thank you, Nero. You may use this place. If Molev looks for me, tell him I went to my village."

"Village?" I just really wanted to sleep.

"My home outside of the city."

Outside of the city meant closer to the wall and the way home, so I didn't argue.

We left the burl, and I closed my eyes, ready for the trip down. The wind continued after we stopped descending. I opened my eyes, anyway.

"How long will it take to get there?"

"Not long. Close your eyes. Rest."

I wouldn't have thought rest possible but managed some, until the steady motion of Drav's running stopped abruptly.

Pulled from my light doze, I opened my eyes and found my head felt a little better. It probably had something to do with the lack of light. We'd stopped close to the wall. No lanterns hung nearby, and the dim light from the larger cluster of crystals suspended above the now distant grove didn't reach far over the fields that stretched out behind us.

Turning my head, I focused on the four stone huts we faced. The structures seemed to emerge from the city wall. Nothing about them looked inviting, except their completely vacated state.

Drav walked to the one on the far left. Once again, no door or covering protected the entrance. Drav's village home didn't look much different than the city dwelling. The builders had used stone to create seating along the walls. Other than the entrance, there were no other openings to see beyond the immediate area just inside the door.

"Stay here, and I'll get a lantern so you can see."

He gently placed me on the bench and left me sitting in the dark. I didn't really mind. It gave me a minute to think.

Resting my head against the stone, I considered everything I'd learned after the arrival of the remainder of Drav's people. The bombings decimating the surface weren't happening worldwide. It gave me hope there might be something left to call home when we returned to the surface.

The news about the infected still roaming didn't surprise me.

I thought of my family and wondered how they were surviving. Were they eating canned dog food? I hoped not. I hoped jackasses like those at the bridge weren't taking all the supplies from the cities and starving out the survivors.

I also hoped the rest of my headache would go away after a nap so we could leave.

Soft light preceded Drav's return and cast enough of a subdued glow to see the rest of the room. I groaned just as he entered.

"Are you in pain?" he asked in concern, moving to my side.

"I'm going to be. Do we really have to sleep on that?" I asked, pointing at the stone bed protruding from the back wall. A furred hide covered the center of the platform with a thickly woven matt at one end.

"You didn't really sleep on there, did you?"

He glanced at the bed.

"Yes," he said, meeting my gaze.

"We must seem like a bunch of marshmallows to you."

"I don't understand."

"Soft and weak."

He feathered a finger over the curve of my cheek.

"Soft, yes. Not weak. Fragile."

I turned my head to kiss his hand.

"Good answer."

He grunted, set the lantern aside, and sat beside me. Leaning into him, I stared at the stone slab, and imagined all the nights he'd lain there. How long would I call his place home?

"I might never see a real bed again," I said quietly. "All those bombs...I wonder if they'll really stop with the cities. Will it be towns next? What will be left when they're done?" I exhaled heavily. "Probably piles of stone and ash. And, I bet there will still be infected."

"Yes. But I will keep you safe."

Of course he would, because we'd be together up there. I patted his leg and lifted my head, looking around at the few items resting on the opposite bench and hung from pegs protruding from the rock. Three hardened gourd looking things hung from a leather strap. Several woven baskets were stacked upside down underneath them.

There wouldn't be much to leave behind when we left.

"Has this place always been your home?"

"Yes."

"You don't have much. Not that it's a bad thing, but you've been here a long time. I thought you would have collected more stuff."

"I don't need anything more than what I have right now." He said the words while sliding his fingers up my arm.

I smiled slightly and leaned against his shoulder once more. His considerate attentiveness made my chest ache in a sweet way. Yet, as much as I wanted to return the sentiment that I had everything I needed, I couldn't. Although I did need Drav, I also needed to get back to the surface, too. I wouldn't just abandon my family.

A yawn broke through, and Drav suggested I lay down.

"I will look for some covers and return soon."

I went to the bed and lay down on the hide. The barrier didn't cushion me from the stone, but it did stop the cold from seeping into my bones.

Closing my eyes, I willed my partial headache away, along with the thoughts of Kristin, Dawn, Mom and Dad, and Ryan.

CHAPTER SIXTEEN

A HOWL PENETRATED MY TROUBLED DREAMS. IN THAT PLACE between asleep and awake, I thought it just my imagination and snuggled more closely to Drav. Then, I heard it again. Long and low, the howl echoed nearby. I jolted upright with a gasp.

Baying and barking began in a frenzy. Drav sighed and sat up with me.

"Did they get inside?" I asked, my heart pounding.

"No. They are outside the wall."

Focusing beyond my racing pulse and panting breaths, I listened. Those hounds didn't sound outside the wall. They sounded like they were only yards away.

"How do you know?" I whispered.

"Because we aren't dead."

I smacked him.

"That is not reassuring."

A horrible scraping reverberated through the stone near

my head. I squeaked and looked at the wall. The scraping, snarling, and howling grew louder.

"They're right on the other side, aren't they?"

Drav ran a soothing hand down my arm.

"Yes. They have very sharp hearing."

"Shit."

"I'm sorry, Mya. I didn't mean to frighten you. They truly are outside the wall and can't get in."

I could barely think over all the noise they were making.

"Are you sure?"

"I'll show you."

He picked me up and had me outside before I could say "no, thank you." With a leap, he jumped onto his hut's roof. A rackety looking scaffolding, made out of branches the size of my wrist, extended up to the top of the wall.

"Would you like me to carry you over my shoulder or climb by yourself?"

I swallowed my first choice of answer—neither—and said I would climb.

He followed closely, his fingers brushing my ankles and guiding me to the next secure footing. At the top, I stood on the lashed branches and peeked over the edge. I couldn't see a thing at first. Then Drav uncovered a lantern that had been placed on the thick stone ledge.

Yips and yowls sounded below as dozens of hellhounds retreated into the darkness beyond the lantern light.

"We can leave this lantern uncovered until the city crystals brighten again."

As he spoke, red dots moved in the distance like a swarm of angry fireflies.

"There are so many out there," I said softly.

"Not so many, but enough. They must be returning from the surface, as well."

I frowned as I considered what that meant. My family would be safer with the hounds down here, but how would we possibly make it back to the surface now? Drav remained quiet a moment when I voiced my concern.

"Returning will be difficult," he said.

"But we're still returning, right?"

He stared out at the sea of red dots for a long while before answering.

"If it is safe, we will return to the surface."

"What? Bullshit. Not 'if it is safe.' It will never be safe again if you guys don't get your asses up there and do something about the mess those things made," I jabbed a finger in the direction of the hellhounds, ignoring the throb of pain growing behind my eyes. "I am going back to the surface, Drav, as soon as it's light again."

However, that didn't happen. The next time the cavern's crystal brightened, my head hurt too much to move more than a few steps on my own.

For two rest periods, we stayed at Drav's village. Not that I got much rest. With mournful howls and aggressive snarls, the hounds rallied outside the wall each time the city crystals dimmed. Drav brought more of the crystal lanterns to line the wall, but it only stopped them from scratching the stone near my head. They knew we were there and wanted in.

My headache and poor mood grew worse. Drav patiently rubbed my head or back through the worst of it and removed the lights from the hut so we sat in the dark. Usually, it helped. But it never lasted.

"I think something's wrong with me," I said in the dark. The city lights hadn't yet dimmed so I lay in the warmth of Drav's arms, relaxing as he played with my hair.

"What do you mean?" With each new headache, his worry for me had only increased.

"I've never gotten headaches like these before. Not one right after the other. I think being down here is making me sick. Humans are supposed to have sunlight. It keeps us healthy."

"You're not eating much," he said. "Perhaps that is the reason."

"I'm not eating because I'll throw up if I do. My head hurts too much."

"Does it hurt now?"

"Not as much when we're laying in the dark. It hurts a lot when I try to move around, or we would have left already." I sighed and tried not to think about the passing time. Instead, I focused on the feel of his hands on my head.

"It feels good when you run your fingers through my hair."

He grunted and kept doing it. I didn't know how his arms never tired, but I sure appreciated his stamina.

"Close your eyes and rest before the hounds come."

THE PAIN in my head pulsed in time with the beat of my heart before I even fully woke. Groaning, I gagged and rolled to the side just in time. Nothing came up but bile because I hadn't eaten since the prior resting period. I lifted my head and tried to open my eyes. The light from a crystal the size of three basketballs pierced my skull. I closed my eyes and swallowed back another urge to gag. That light needed to go.

Through sheer determination, I lifted myself from the slab, dragging a blanket with me. Step by painful step, I approached the mini moon in the center of the hut.

My attempt to flip the blanket over the crystal threw me off balance, and I fell forward and landed against the crystal. Pain lanced through me like a thousand needles had pierced me at once. I screamed.

"Mya! Mya!"

Drav's voice pulled me from the darkness into the excruciating light. My skin felt raw and bruised, and the touch of his arms when he attempted to lift me made me want to die.

"Stop," I begged with tears burning my throat.

"Please don't cry. Tell me what's wrong."

I swallowed a gag and panted in pain.

"Take the crystal out," I managed between breaths.

He immediately set me on my side of the bed. Every

movement, no matter how gentle, hurt. He made soothing sounds, and the light disappeared. Curled in a ball of misery, I breathed in and out, focusing on the cool rock beneath me. A hot spot on my side where I landed on the crystal was flush against the rock, easing the sting a miniscule amount.

"Mya?" Drav said softly. "Are you hurt?"

His fingers gently smoothed over my hair.

"I hurt all over."

"Can I bring a lantern in to check you?"

"No." The idea of being near a crystal made my stomach turn. "No more crystals. Every time I'm near one for too long, the headaches get worse. I accidently touched the big one and thought I was going to die. They're making me sick, Drav. I need to leave."

"Are you sure it's the crystals?"

"Yes."

He stroked my hair for several quiet minutes before speaking again.

"We need to return to the city."

I groaned. The idea of going anywhere just now made me want to puke. Yet the idea of waiting longer filled me with a certainty that I was going to die down here.

"Why? Why can't we just leave?" My eyes started to tear up. "Why are you doing this?"

"We will need help."

He slid his arm under me, attempting to pick me up, and I cried out. He immediately stopped.

"Can we wait a little while?" I panted. "How much time until the hounds get here?"

"Not long."

"Let's rest until then."

He lay beside me, his heat warming and soothing me. With a sigh, I relaxed against him and waited for the throbbing in my head to ease up.

It never did.

Drav's fingers rubbed the base of my skull. The kneading movement had eased some of the pain before, but it didn't help now.

"Drav," a voice called from outside.

I groaned at the sound. The voice called again, and Drav slipped from the bed.

"I will be back."

He left and spoke softly to his visitor.

The howls of the hounds started and pierced my skull. Knowing that it would be time for us to go soon anyway, I slowly sat up. My body ached all over. My stomach rolled as I swung my legs over the edge of the bed. I paused to take a few steadying breaths.

"Mya." Drav stepped back into the house, his body silhouetted the entrance way. He rushed over when I pushed off the bed, trying to get to my feet.

"How do you feel?"

"Terrible."

I shivered. Drav frowned, and I brought my hand to his cheek.

"I need to get away from the crystals," I said. "I need to go home."

"Yes. Ghua has returned from the surface. He will

accompany us to the city."

"I thought we could skip that part," I said, glancing at Ghua, who had followed Drav in.

"No, Mya. We need help to reach the surface safely."

Of course. He was right. How could he defend me from a hound when he had to carry me?

"Okay, we can go. But, I'm not sure I'll be able to stand up."

Drav didn't waste another second before he had me in his arms. He looked down at me, gauging my reaction to being held. I ached but tried not to show it.

"I'm fine," I said.

Drav's gaze swept over my face once more before he stepped out of the hut to where Ghua now waited for us. Ghua had a couple of scratches on his arms that were healing and a multitude of scrapes and bruises on the exposed skin of his shirtless chest.

"Hey, Ghua. What the hell happened to you?" I asked.

"Hounds."

Just more evidence of how much help we would need to travel through hound infested caverns.

"Why did you return so much later than everyone else?" I asked.

Ghua smiled, his canines flashing. He had a twinkle of mischief in his eyes, but not before his smile dropped and sorrow replaced it.

"There is much news."

"Come. We will return to the city, share the news, and see

who will join us," Drav said, leading the way with me in his arms.

He and Ghua spoke softly in their language as we traveled. It didn't bother me anymore. Nothing bothered me but my head, stomach, and the clawing need to get back to the surface.

Ghua glanced at me a couple of times, his gaze filled with sympathy and worry.

"Mya, okay?" Ghua asked.

"No, not really."

The pain and sickness grew progressively worse the closer we got to the city due to the lanterns that lit the pathway every ten feet. My stomach began to cramp so badly I wrapped an arm around my middle. Drav caught the move and watched me with increasing concern.

"Just get us there and get us help," I said softly.

Within the towering timbers, the city seemed to be a flurry of activity. Others hurried past us, some nodding in acknowledgement, some carrying weapons and travel bags over their shoulders. A few stared at me, curious, but most seemed to have become accustom to my presence. I could have sworn I even heard a couple say a few things in English.

Drav and Ghua quieted as we drew near the common area. The low tones of Molev's distant voice drilled into my brain. I rested my head against Drav's chest, my achy body tired and demanding more sleep. I didn't sleep, but I shut my eyes in the hopes that the pounding in my head would calm. Or even that my stomach stopped twisting in knots. Anything to give me some type of relief.

"Mya," a familiar voice said, much too loudly.

I opened my eyes to see we'd reached the lantern lit common area. Molev stood in the center of a large gathering and waved us forward through the crowd, closer into the heart of the poisonous light.

Although packed with hot bodies, the area felt cold. Cold enough that I exhaled to test if I could see my breath. Struggling not to shiver uncontrollably in Drav's arms, I closed my eyes briefly and swallowed down my bile.

"You do not look well, Mya," Molev said.

"She's not," Drav said, answering for me. "The crystals are making her sick. She needs to return to the surface."

"Are you certain it's the crystals?" Molev asked.

"Just coming here has made her worse. Before this, she accidentally touched the large guard crystal I'd taken inside the hut before bringing it to the wall. She fell over after touching it."

"I think I'm dying," I whispered.

As if reacting to my words, shivers wracked my body.

"We need more time," Molev said. "Another rest for those who just returned to be ready."

"We don't have more time. Look at her. We need to leave now."

Molev grunted, and Drav held me more firmly to his chest.

"Those who are ready," Molev said loudly, "will leave now. Those who are not ready will meet us on the surface in one rest. We also need men to stay and guard the city. If the

humans do not welcome us as Mya has, we will need a place
we can return to."

"What of Merdon and Ririn, and the four who have not
returned?" Ghua asked.

"We will search for them when we reach the surface and
hope our brothers aren't gone, and the traitors are."

A universal agreement ran through the crowd.

"Drav, please," I rasped. Everything hurt so much.
Talking. Thinking. Even breathing.

"We leave now," Molev said. "The return of the hounds
will make the journey dangerous. Be ready."

The crowd, who had been quiet, broke out in a hub of
noise.

The racket added to the pain, and I whimpered. My
stomach cramped painfully, and a gag caught in my throat.

"Mya?"

"I don't feel well, Drav," I mumbled. "It's so cold here."

His lips touched my forehead.

"You are not cold. You're hot," he said.

Figured. Fever in hell. Part of me frowned at that
thought. Not hell. Drav's home.

"You're hotter than you've ever been. Your heart is
racing."

I gagged again.

"What do I do, Mya?"

"Fevers need to be cooled. But it won't help. We need to
leave. It's the crystals."

Drav ran.

CHAPTER SEVENTEEN

EACH STRIDE RATTLED MY TEETH, DESPITE MY CLENCHED JAW.
Never in my life had I felt so cold or hurt so much. I could
barely think past the pounding in my skull. It just needed to
end. Now.

"P-please, just r-rip my head off," I stuttered to Drav.

"No, Mya. You will die."

"I'm already dying."

He growled fiercely and ran faster. I burrowed my face in
his shirt, desperate for some heat. Some relief. Tears gathered
as I thought what would happen if I died. My family would
be left always wondering what had happened.

We suddenly stopped moving.

"I'm sorry, Mya."

That was all the warning Drav gave before he jumped.
Icy spears lanced through me as we plunged into the river.
The shock of it kept me from gasping until our heads popped
back up.

I choked on a curse and shivered uncontrollably.

"Just a little longer," Drav whispered in my ear, holding me when I would have flailed in the direction of the bank. "We need to cool you."

If I'd thought the air cold before, the water robbed me of every ounce of heat, sucking my energy until I could barely cling to Drav. His lips brushed my forehead, cheek, and mouth.

"You're cooling. Hold your breath one more time."

"N-n-no."

"Three. Two."

I inhaled quickly and held it.

"One."

He dunked us under again. I wouldn't have thought my head held any warmth after the first submersion. However, I was proven wrong the second time the icy water enveloped us and stole what remained of my heat and strength.

We broke the surface, and Drav surged out of the water onto the bank. Cradling me in his arms, he sat and gently rocked me. Some of the pain in my head had eased. That or the water had numbed it. For a moment, I let myself float in the almost nothingness that waited at the edge of my consciousness.

Drav's hands wiped over my face, and his lips brushed mine repeatedly between softly spoken pleas for me to open my eyes.

I felt so tired. Yet, hearing his gruff demanding voice, I forced myself to try. As soon as I opened my eyes, he kissed me hard.

"Do not do that again," he said when he pulled away.

"T-that's my l-line."

He hugged me close, melting my anger with his body heat. We stayed like that until the worst of my tremors stopped. In the darkness by the river, the pain in my head didn't return full-force. It didn't fade either. A steady thumping persisted, reminding me that we needed to leave these caverns, no matter what.

In the distance, the faint sounds of baying echoed. Between the crystal poisoning and the gathered hounds, the journey to the surface wouldn't be an easy one.

"Drav, I need you to promise me something."

"Anything."

"If something happens to me, you need to find my family and tell them everything. From the moment we met until the end. Except for the boob grabbing and kissing. That would upset my parents."

"Nothing will happen to you," he said, before pressing another kiss to my temple.

"Drav, I'm sick, and we still have caverns filled with hellhounds to fight our way through. If something happens, I want your word you will try to find my family. I have a picture of them in my bag. I know it's asking a lot, but I can't leave them just wondering. And, they need your help to live."

"Nothing will happen, Mya. You will see your family again. I give you my word."

I sighed and closed my eyes, knowing that was as good as I'd get from him. The stubborn man wouldn't give up on the idea of both of us making it to the surface alive and well. What would happen then?

"It's not going to be easy once we reach the top," I said. "The infected will still be roaming. The hounds will likely follow us. And, everyone will probably want to kill you." I rubbed my head against his wet shirt. "I wish there was a safe place for us to just...be."

"We will find a place. Your world is very large."

"It is. And a lot emptier now. Maybe we can find a farm in the middle of nowhere. We can grow things like you do down here. Maybe even raise chickens or something...if we can find any."

"We can do anything you want, as long as we're together."

I lifted my head and met his worried gaze.

"Together," I agreed, ignoring the sinking feeling in my stomach.

He kissed me softly then tucked my back against his chest. We stayed like that until Molev found us a while later.

"We are ready. Is Mya all right?"

Drav stood with me in his arms.

"For now. I will meet you at the gate. We can't risk lit caverns. Mya grows too sick in the light."

"But the hounds."

"I know. Make sure to let everyone know what we face and that any lanterns must stay away from Mya."

Molev glanced at me. Was he wondering if I was worth all the trouble? I hoped not because I couldn't think of a reason to support my worth at the moment.

"We will meet you at the gate," he said finally. "We will keep you safe, Mya."

"Thank you. Can someone bring my bag? It has things in it that I still need." Mostly, the picture of my family. Just in case.

"I will bring it," Molev said.

Drav set off at a run. The breeze made me shiver, but I didn't complain about the wet clothing. The cold helped numb the body aches. Closing my eyes, I tried to rest. It worked until we reached the outer wall. The sound of Drav's running attracted the hounds on the other side. Snarls and growls increased in volume and number as he ran.

"Maybe we should run through the fields," I said.

"No. The light will hurt you."

"So will all the hellhounds that are following us to the gate."

Drav grunted and glanced at the fields. The lantern light didn't hurt my eyes, but it would hurt my head once we drew closer.

"It'll be a good test to see how close I can be to the lanterns when we're out there. Better to know now when we're safe, right?"

My reasoning seemed to decide him. He veered inward and wove his way between the lanterns. The baying fell behind, remaining near the point of the wall where they'd last heard us.

"How do you feel?" Drav asked after passing by several lanterns. He kept at least ten feet away.

"It's not getting any worse when we move between the

ones with smaller pieces of crystals. I can feel the ones with bigger chunks, though."

He pressed his lips to my forehead.

"You're starting to warm again."

The hot grittiness I'd felt in my eyes hadn't returned since our plunge in the water, so I couldn't be too bad, yet. A sudden thought occurred to me, and I jerked my head up to stare at Drav. The move made my head pound a little more noticeably.

"If I get too warm again, promise you won't jump in any fish infested waters to cool me off once we're outside the wall."

"I promise I will care for you and keep you safe."

I set my head back on his chest.

"Not the promise I was looking for."

He kissed the top of my head.

"Rest. Sleep while you can."

Unfortunately, I hurt enough that resting proved impossible. But I closed my eyes and pretended for his peace of mind.

While he ran, I listened to the sounds of the hounds fade and swell in waves. Although I knew he stayed in the fields, based on the pain I experienced from the nearby lanterns, the creatures still gathered at places outside the walls. Probably near the tiny village stations the men used to guard their city. I could only imagine how many hounds we would have attracted if we'd stayed running near the wall. Hopefully, my suffering now would keep us safer when we left. And I certainly did suffer. The pulsing energy from each crystal seemed to burrow into my bones and twist me from the inside.

By the time we reached the gate, my stomach churned nauseatingly; and the sounds of the hounds outside grew.

"Do you have her water bottle?" Drav asked, slowing.

I opened my eyes to see a large gathering of men before us. Those nearest the gate held lanterns, glowing with large chunks of crystals. I could feel the energy from where we stood and winced. Drav caught the look and stepped further away. The men not carrying the lanterns held bows and spears. Some had knives strapped to their legs.

Molev moved forward. He carried a spear along with my bag.

"I thought you only used your weapons for hunting," I said, the words coming out slightly slurred.

He handed me the bottle.

"I'm not thirsty," I said.

"You need to drink, Mya. Please," Drav said.

I sighed and took a tiny sip before passing the bottle back.

"Leaving with lanterns is usually enough to keep the hounds away. However, we generally hunt in the crystal caverns. This time, we will travel through the dark ones. We will need both the lanterns and the weapons to keep you safe."

"You say that as if you don't like the idea of killing them." The effort of the words had me closing my eyes briefly.

"Because, even with weapons, we can't kill them. We can only slow them and make it take longer for them to heal."

Leaving the city walls should have terrified me. Instead, I only felt relief. We were finally making our way to the surface. To my family. To the survivors who needed our help.

Drav looked up at the men. "The larger crystals poison her quicker. She can endure the smaller from a distance."

Molev nodded.

"You will carry her at our center. Those with the lanterns will form a circle around us in the open caves. In the tunnels and cross ways, the lanterns will move to the front and the back. Those of us with spears will guard the lantern bearers. Those with arrows will remain closest to Drav and Mya."

I shivered slightly in Drav's arms.

"We must leave," he said. "She's warming again. No stopping. No rests."

"No rests? Won't you get tired?" I asked.

He met my worried gaze.

"Resting in dark caves is too dangerous, and I fear what resting in crystal caves would do to you."

All good points, which made me feel guilty as hell.

"If you get tired, don't be stubborn. Ask someone else to carry me for a bit."

He grunted, and I knew he'd never willingly let someone else carry me.

"Are you ready?" Molev asked.

Drav nodded. The two men by the gate removed the brace. The barking outside the wall grew more intense. Two other men scurried up the ladders and uncovered lanterns on top of the wall. Yipping and snarls drew further away, and the men by the gate started pulling the rock slab open. Those with lanterns crowded near the gap.

In the darkness beyond, I could see the multitude of glowing red eyes, and my heart started to thump heavily in my chest.

"I will keep you safe," Drav vowed, pressing a kiss to my head.

I said nothing, just watched the first of the lantern carriers slip outside the wall followed by the men with spears. When more than half the group had left, the rest stood aside. Drav walked forward. I closed my eyes against the feel of the crystals on the wall as we passed through the opening. Part of me considered keeping them closed, but I had to know what we faced. What I saw terrified me.

A sea of blinking red dots circled our group, kept at bay by the weak light of the lanterns and the sharp ends of spears. As Drav moved forward, so too did the lantern bearers at the front.

"Is everyone out?" Molev asked. He held a position near the front, spear in hand.

"Yes," someone said from behind us. I looked back and saw we stood in the center of a lantern circle. The gate rumbled closed behind us, and the lanterns disappeared from the top of the wall.

"We run and we don't stop," Molev said.

CHAPTER EIGHTEEN

Dᴬᴠ ꜱᴛᴀʀᴛᴇᴅ ʀᴜɴɴɪɴɢ ᴀɴᴅ ᴛʜᴇ ꜱɪxᴛʏ ᴍᴇɴ ᴀʀᴏᴜɴᴅ ᴜꜱ moved with him, a protective barrier against the growing mass of writhing black bodies hungry for flesh.

A hound, keeping pace just outside the circle of light, darted in toward a lantern carrier. The creature screamed in pain as the crystal's glow bathed its coarse fur, but didn't stop its charge. The carrier saw it coming. His gait remained steady until the last possible second when he jumped mid-stride. A spear pierced the hound's side. The spear bearer, who I hadn't noticed, hoisted the hound and threw it off the end of the spear into the dark.

Seeing one of their own wounded and tossed aside sent the rest into a frenzy. The baying and snarls grew deafening. More darted in, attempting to bring down the lantern bearers and extinguish the light. The men with bows and spears kept the hounds at bay.

Molev yelled something into the din, but I couldn't make it out.

A moment later, two of the lantern bearers at the front moved closer to each other while the next two stopped altogether. It took a second to understand why. We were running through two enormous columns. The two who'd stayed behind stood on the outside of the columns, keeping the darkness and hounds back as the rest passed through.

After the columns, nothing separated us from the first dark cavern. Almost as if the hounds sensed they were losing their prey, half their number darted forward toward the abyss.

"Do not let them reach the cavern first," Molev yelled.

Drav tensed and leaned into his run, picking up speed. The lantern bearers in the front did their best to reach the cavern entrance first, but missed it by at least a dozen hounds. Red eyes glowed in the darkness ahead as the men continued forward. The men waved the lanterns, forcing the hounds back. The hoarse yowls echoed around us as the light hit them.

The hounds behind kept a healthy distance from the crystals, not that I blamed them. The lanterns, even though a distance from me, still made my head ache and my stomach twist.

Despite the agony it caused them, a few hell hounds charged forward, sharp, yellowed teeth flashing in the green light before a spear or arrow whistled through the air. A meaty thud followed. The men kept their pace, veering to the right, out of the dark lush sub cavern and into the barren cool darkness of a cavern void of crystals.

Although I felt an immediate degree of relief, I couldn't enjoy it. I knew where we were. This stark cavern belonged to the hounds.

A pained yell came from behind us. I itched to glance over Drav's shoulder, but his words stopped me.

"Do not look back, Mya. He will rise at the pool and join the others."

I heeded Drav's warning and lay my head back on his shoulder. The fever still lingered, and I felt exhausted. Drav held me securely against him, but it didn't stop the throbbing pain that shot through my head with each stride. Although, the darkness eased the worst of my pain, the crystal lanterns that surrounded us guaranteed my fever would slowly return.

Drav misstepped and lurched forward. Bile rose to the back of my throat at the movement, and I fought not to throw up.

"Are you all right?" he asked, not stopping.

"Yes. If you need the lanterns closer—"

"No. I can see well enough. There's another entrance ahead."

The men picked up speed together and raced for it, creating distance between us and the pack of hellhounds.

As soon as we emerged from the other end of the passageway, all sounds of pursuit abruptly ceased. I shivered and wondered what that meant while I struggled to see where we were.

This cavern, too, had no crystals. The absence of that

stronger light continued to prevent the pain in my head from increasing, despite the smaller green shards around us. However, those shards proved too small for the complete nothingness in this cave.

The darkness swam in, like an unsuspecting fog. It rolled around us until we were submerged. From the echoing glow of the furthest crystal, I could only see shadows outlining Drav's chest and my hand, if I brought it close enough to my face.

The silence settled around us. Even with the sound of the men's feet hitting the compact floor, the quiet heightened my anxiety.

A hollow howl suddenly came from behind us a moment before the burst of noise echoed off the stone walls. The never-ending sound boomed in my ears. I stiffened in Drav's arms, but he didn't even flinch. The hounds had entered the cavern and passed through whatever barrier had kept their pursuit quiet from us.

A few of the lanterns swayed haphazardly before I spotted the first set of red eyes.

The hounds surged forward, a mass of angry predators closing in on their prey. The first scream made me jump. More yells from the men who fought filled the cavern.

I watched another lantern bearer fall away into the dark. The man behind him, ran faster to fill in the space and close the circle around us.

"Keep moving forward," Molev called out from nearby.

The men didn't stop running. But the darkness remained unchanged as if we didn't make any progress at all. Slinking shapes kept pace in the lanterns glow. Exaggerated shadows of the hounds stretched and twisted. One moment, there; the next, gone.

The men switched directions, avoiding the shadows when they appeared. An arrow whistled in the air, and I tucked myself closer to Drav.

Two men suddenly went down, seemingly yanked into the darkness by nothing. A howl followed their disappearance. There were shouts from the back of the group, and we began to slow down. The scrape of nails against the stone ground and heavy panting surrounded us.

I peeked over Drav's shoulder and saw a flash of red eyes. The hounds were herding our group, trying to separate us from the two who had fallen.

"Keep moving," Molev called out again, his voice heavy with regret.

One of the men let out a cry cut off by a wet gurgle. I shuddered, knowing the sound would haunt me in my nightmares.

"The men will return to the pool, inside the city. They will be safe," Drav said.

"Will they remember their deaths?"

Drav didn't answer, and I knew they would. Being ripped apart by a hound would be a terrible thing to remember for eternity.

The hounds' efforts grew more intense in the next cavern.

Molev ran up next to Drav and spoke to him quietly in their language. I hated that they were keeping things from me, but I was still too tired to protest.

"No," Drav said firmly.

"What's going on?" I asked.

"Molev wishes to take a detour through one of the lit caverns."

I thought of the number of hounds following us and the men we'd lost. They were picking us off slowly. It would only be a matter of time before the hounds tried something braver. Although I understood the fallen men weren't really dead, the thought of Kerr, Shax, or Ghua getting hurt before we reached the surface worried me.

And then, of course, there was Drav. The thought of something bad happening to him broke me. I couldn't bear it. If his safety meant I would have to be in a bit more discomfort for a while, I could stand it.

Besides, the men were the ones that would get me to the surface. Without them, I would be lost.

"It's the smartest idea."

"No, you are still hot."

"I'll be okay. All these dark caves have helped. Passing through a light cave will win us some safety and breathing room. I promise to tell you the moment I start to feel worse."

Molev ran next to us, listening to our conversation.

"If Mya is okay with it, the men could use a rest."

I didn't know how long we had run. It was impossible to tell in the darkness. But after losing men, I could understand the group's wariness to continue.

"I can handle it for a while," I said to Drav, who nodded to Molev.

Molev called out, and the group changed directions.

Hounds darted forward, trying to catch the outermost runners with a bite. Those within the circle let arrows fly into the rushing hounds.

"Almost there," Drav said.

Turning forward, I saw a lit cavern in the distance. Sparse vegetation grew on the outskirts of where the illumination reached. Jackalopes sprinted from the growth toward the light before we even came close, the baying alerting them of the danger.

I squinted against the increasing brightness. The men raced forward, the lantern holders moving to the side to let those without light through first.

Drav rushed into the passage with the rest following, and I exhaled in relief at the hounds' wailing at the loss of prey.

"Are you all right?" Drav asked, slowing.

"Yes. So far so good." And I was. The cavern wasn't as huge as the city's, meaning the crystals in the ceiling were smaller, too. Although my head still thumped, the pain didn't seem to grow terribly worse.

As a group, we made our way through the well-lit cavern's thick vegetation to the center. Men plopped to the ground, sides heaving.

"Can you put me down, please?" I asked, knowing Drav had to be tired, too.

He eased me to my feet but kept a hold on my arms. The support kept me steady on my numb legs.

"Mya?"

"Hmm?"

"How do you feel?"

"I'm okay for now. Honest. How much longer until we reach the old orchard?" I asked, my gaze drifting to the men around us. Molev walked among them, speaking to a few here and there.

"Not long," Drav answered. "One more resting period."

"Is that how long we ran?"

"No. Not quite half of that."

Crap. Worry pooled in my stomach, and I began to count men.

"We lost seven," Molev said, coming up to us. "The crystals in this cave are still strong. We can rest for a while but should leave well before the light begins to dim." He studied me for a moment. "Are you well?"

"I'm holding it together for the moment. I can feel the crystals, but the run through the dark caves helped settle the worst of it," I lied. "So I should be fine in here for a bit."

"Good. Thank you."

As soon as he walked away, Drav convinced me to sit in the tall grass.

"Stay. I will get your bag. You need to eat and drink something."

"Thank you." The thought of food still didn't appeal to me. However, I kept quiet because Drav would worry if I said something.

A wave of exhaustion swept over me, and my eyelids fell heavily. When Drav returned with food and nudged me, I couldn't bring myself to open my eyes. Splashing of the water and quiet whispers lulled me to sleep.

Drav's warmth left my back a moment before I felt myself lifted into the air.

"She's growing warm again," he said. "We must go."

Around me, I listened to the slight rustle of noise as the men stood and started moving.

"I'm fine," I tried to say, but the words came out a slurred murmur. "They need more rest."

"You are not fine," Drav said. "And we've rested as long as we dare."

I didn't have the energy to argue.

We made our way toward the next cavern's entrance. The sudden temperature drop and complete darkness gave a welcome respite. I hadn't been aware of just how badly my head hurt, until the pain began to ease.

My head and stomach settled enough that I closed my eyes, and I dozed on and off as Drav and his men ran tirelessly through caverns. Occasionally, the volume of Molev's voice would rise and rouse me. But never for long. The steady swaying motion of Drav's gait and the strong sure hold of his arms always pulled me back under, and the much-needed rest worked wonders.

When I next opened my eyes, my head no longer beat in time with my pulse. My stomach didn't feel the greatest, but the sensation of being on the verge of vomiting had faded.

"It seems quieter," I said, glancing up at Drav's tense jaw.

"It is. How are you feeling?"

"Better. My head and stomach only hurt a little."

"Good."

"Do you want to take a break? Could Kerr or Shax carry me for a while?" I asked only because I worried for him. I saw how tired the others had been from running full out. And I didn't want Drav weak or exhausted if the hounds attacked.

"No."

"Please, Drav. I'm okay with it. I don't want you to—"

"Mya, I am fine."

Before I could argue with him, a long, lone howl split the air. It sounded different than the normal baying. Close, but not frenzied.

The men immediately picked up their pace.

"What was that?"

"Hunting call," Molev said from nearby. "It's to let the others know prey has been spotted."

Howls started up around us, all coming from different directions. I twisted in Drav's arms and spotted a looming sea of red in the darkness.

CHAPTER NINETEEN

THE HELL HOUNDS CAME AT US LIKE A SWARM, BLINKING OUT of sight here and there because of the columns hidden within the depths of the cavern.

Ahead, one of the leading lantern bearers said something I didn't understand. However, whatever the guy had shouted couldn't have been good because Molev swore in English.

"Tighten the circle. Channel ahead. Watch from above," he called out.

"Above?" I said.

"We should turn back," Drav shouted to Molev over the baying and snarls.

"If you could look back, you would know that's not an option."

I looked over Drav's shoulder, and my mouth dropped open. Very few of the lanterns remained. Even as I watched, a sleek black body leapt forward and silently brought another man down.

"We can't go back," I said to Drav. "We're running out of lanterns."

He ran faster.

"Close your eyes," he ordered.

My stomach churned with fear. Just what the hell was going to happen? I looked ahead. Numerous stocky columns rose out of the darkness. The hounds racing ahead of us scrabbled up the rocky sides. One reached a peak before we entered the maze of pillars.

From atop its perch, the hound launched itself into the center of our group. Mad eyes fixed on a hunter not far from us, the hound salivated and snarled as it fell. It yelped in pain when the light of the crystals touched it but didn't twist to avoid the brightness.

The hunter hefted his long spear and braced himself. The hound skewered its body onto the pole without a flinch. It clawed at the shaft, trying to pull closer to the hunter. Meanwhile, other hounds were winning their way to the tops of other pillars.

Now I understood why Drav wanted me to close my eyes.

We were all going to die. Only, there was no resurrection pool for me. I clung to Drav as we passed between the first two pillars. Hounds began launching themselves at will, reducing our numbers in seconds. Blood spattered my jean clad legs. As much as I wanted to close my eyes, I couldn't.

This was the cost of returning me to the surface. Closing my eyes to it wouldn't make it any less real.

Screams and roars echoed around us. The thump of the

men's feet on the ground as they ran was non-existent in the noise.

Turning my head, I caught movement high to our right. A hound's eyes met mine from above just as it leapt toward us.

I gasped and cringed into Drav.

"Molev," Drav shouted.

Then he threw me. I screamed, sailing through the air, looking back to see the hound bring Drav down. Another converged on him.

I screamed his name.

Strong arms caught me, and the forward momentum jerked me, interrupting my view. When I saw again, there was nothing but a pile of black bodies where Drav had stood.

"No!" The cry ripped through me. I didn't care if he had resurrected a million times before, I didn't trust fate to bring him back to me now. Not after everything I'd seen.

I looked up at Molev's shadowed face.

"Stop! You have to help him!"

Molev didn't slow. He veered, avoiding another leaping hound.

"Ghua," he yelled.

Yet again, I found myself sailing through the air. Molev shouted out several names as Ghua caught me and tucked me under one arm, carrying me like a flailing football. I lifted my head and squinted at the bright glow of the lantern he carried in his other hand. Four more lantern bearers moved to surround us, all running at the same breakneck pace as

Ghua. The light of the crystals they held, the only thing keeping the beasts at bay.

A shout from behind us distracted the circling, snapping hounds, though. Their numbers thinned, opening a path to the next dimly lit cavern.

"Ghua, please," I panted. "You have to help Drav."

"I am," he said.

He continued forward, toward the dim light of the cavern. As soon as we exploded through the passageway, the noise of the fight behind us couldn't be heard over the sound of the group's harsh breathing. Ghua fell to his knees, taking me with him.

His sides heaved with great, gasping breaths as did those of the men around him.

Ignoring the pounding behind my eyes, I scrambled to my knees and looked back at the black entrance. For a moment, I heard and saw nothing. Then the faint snarls and growls reached me. The hounds were already turning away, knowing the light in the cavern would be too much for them. But, they'd gotten what they'd wanted.

Tears flowed down my cheeks, and a sob caught in my throat. Slowly, I wrapped my arms around my aching middle.

"He will swim in the pool and come back for you, Mya. Do not doubt that." Ghua's hand gripped my shoulder, a small comfort to my breaking world.

None of the men spoke as I continued to cry through my pain. A numbness crept in. I swallowed hard and wiped the back of my hand across my dripping nose. After a few calming breaths, I looked up at Ghua who squatted beside me, studying me with concern.

"How will we ever reach the surface with just the six of us?" I asked, my voice still rough.

"We need to stick to the light caverns."

"That will only work until the old orchard. It and the cavern leading up to the surface are both dark," I said.

He nodded.

"We'll wait until the old orchard is lit. We will be safe. But I will need to carry you and run, Mya."

"I know."

He stood and offered me his hand.

"Come. We must keep moving. The light is increasing here and will give us more time."

I stood and let Ghua pick me up. It wasn't the same as running with Drav. He didn't hold me as closely, for which I felt very grateful.

We ran through the lit cavern, my heart feeling heavier with each step.

A distant sound stopped Ghua before we reached the next entrance. He turned back, looking the way we'd come. I saw nothing in the soft light but the swaying long purple grass. Another anguished howl-like yell echoed distantly.

"Is it the hounds?" I asked, my heart beating hard. They shouldn't have been able to enter, not with the light.

"No," Ghua said. He started walking toward the sound. "It's your name."

I tilted my head and listened. This time, I heard it. The long, drawn out syllables of my name.

"Is it—?" My throat tightened with hope.

"I can't tell." He turned back and started to jog, the other's falling in around us.

From a distance, I caught the shape of four men. Just four out of the sixty who'd left the city with us.

"It's Molev, Drav, Kerr, and Shax," Ghua said.

I started to cry. Ghua picked up the pace, and we met them near the base of one of the spindly trees. I pushed myself from his arms and went running to Drav, who was being half carried, half dragged by Molev and Shax. Blood covered every inch of his skin, along with bites and ripped, gaping wounds. He seemed blind as he yelled my name again, and swung his head from side to side.

"She's right in front of you. Stop your yelling," Molev said. He released Drav, who fell to the ground.

I ran to him.

"Does anyone have my bag?"

Kerr set it beside me. His bloody hand caught my attention. I looked up and noticed, in a glance, they all looked just about as bad as Drav.

"You heal faster in the caverns, right?" I asked.

Molev collapsed to the ground beside Drav.

"Yes. We will need a rest period. Maybe two."

I grabbed my water bottle and dribbled some onto Drav's ravaged face. His eyes were too swollen to tell if he really had been blinded.

"Everything will heal?" I asked, worried.

"Yes. We keep the scars until we are reborn."

"Mya," Drav gasped, his hand reaching up and closing around mine.

"I'm here," I said, afraid to touch him. "Lie down. I'll lie with you."

"No. Must leave. Crystals."

"It'll be okay," I said, giving him a gentle nudge. "Ghua is here and will wake us before I get sick. It'll be just enough time to let you heal."

Drav eased down to the ground and pulled me close. His bleeding had already stopped. Within seconds, he slept.

I looked up at Ghua, my head already pounding. However, I couldn't be sure if it was from the scare and the tears or the crystals.

"Don't wake them up until everyone can run. None of us will survive if we have to carry the injured."

He nodded slowly, and I closed my eyes.

SOMETHING cold and wet pressed against my forehead, and I tried to push it away. I could barely lift my arm, though.

"Mya?"

"Stop." My word slurred with sleep.

"Mya, you must wake."

"No, too tired."

Drav shook me lightly.

"Your fever is back. You must wake."

"Stop, I'm awake."

"Then open your eyes."

With a great effort, I managed to crack my eyelids open a bit. The light was gone, replaced with darkness again. A lantern was nearby, and I cringed away from it.

"We are getting close to the crater. We need to keep moving, Drav," Molev said from somewhere right beside me. Drav pulled away the cloth he was using to wipe down my forehead. How long had I been out? I groaned from the pain radiating in my body.

"Ghua is going to lift you. Are you ready to move again?"

Honestly, I wanted to tell him no, I wasn't. But, I knew I wouldn't be getting any better here. A hound howled, and it sounded too close for comfort. Ghua picked me up as gently as he could, but the fever and the accompanying pain made everything worse. I bit back my cry of pain and turned my head to look at Drav.

His face looked less swollen. But, when he stood, he did so with a grimace and stepped back with a limp.

"You need more rest," I said.

"I'm sorry, Mya," Ghua said. "You do not look well. I had to wake them."

He took off running, and the agony that jolted in my head pulled me into a pain-filled darkness.

"We are close."

"She needs help."

"Once we get to the surface, we will find her people. Someone will help her."

Drav and Molev's conversation grated on my nerves. Every sound seemed heightened, and I wanted them to stop talking.

I groaned and tried to open one eyelid. I only caught a glimpse of our surroundings before it closed. Darkness surrounded us, but the ceiling had seemed familiar. I tried again, and Drav noticed.

"She is awake. We must move now," Molev called out.

Drav held me tightly, his fingers running through my hair. I wanted to ask what was wrong, but he had me up in his arms before I could.

"You must hold onto me."

I did as he asked but had no strength in my grip. Drav ran forward and there was a pressure in my ears as they popped loudly and painfully. I winced. We'd just passed through the barrier. We were almost there.

I spontaneously threw up on myself, and weakly choked on it.

"You will be okay, Mya. You will be."

Muscles moved under me. I drifted off, knowing he was wrong this time.

Molev's quiet voice roused me again. Something was tied around me, anchoring me to Drav.

"Drav," I rasped. "Remember. Family. Promise."

"I remember, Mya. I promise you will see them again."

I wouldn't. I couldn't see anything. But, I tried again to open my eyes.

Just when I thought it wasn't working, I saw the stars. They glittered above me with a dazzling beauty rarely seen even at the cabin. I wanted to cry. The twinkling stars above us seemed too spectacular to be true. My fever had to be making me delusional.

"We are here," Drav said, untying me. He lay me on the cool ground. Instead of stars, I stared up at his ravaged face.

"Where?" I rasped.

"The surface," he said.

I sighed and closed my eyes. He'd done it. He'd returned me to the surface like I'd asked. But far too late.

"Thank you, Drav. Don't forget your promise."

With that, I let the darkness take me once more, barely hearing Drav's anguished cry.

"No, Mya! I will not lose you."

Thank you for reading Demon Flames! The story continues in Demon Ash, the third book in the Resurrection Chronicles. Now Available!

AUTHOR'S NOTE

Don't hate us for that ending! We promise the next one won't end like that and hope you'll continue the journey with us. Our world destruction is just getting going!

We'd love to hear what you're thinking of the series so far! Just leave a review on the retailer site of your choice. Reviews are so important to spread the word about a story you loved or hated. Also, tell a friend about the series! Word of mouth recommendations are even better than reviews. (Maybe even better than pizza, wine, and cheesecake…maybe.)

To ensure you never miss a release, please consider subscribing to MJ's Newsletter. (She'll only send periodically, so you won't be overwhelmed.)

Until next time!

Melissa and Becca

SNEAK PEEK OF DEMON ASH

Now Available!

Everything hurt. The steady throbbing in my skull penetrated my disoriented mind, creating a dark dreamscape filled with terrors I didn't believe real. Skeletal black bodies with glowing red eyes swarmed around us. A single flashlight and four spear-bearing men with grey skin kept them at bay. A man with a mangled face whispered that I would have no second life, that I needed to cling to the first.

I didn't want to cling to anything. Pain enveloped me when I tried. So I let go, but I couldn't drift.

The clamor of sound, echoing howls and incomprehensible shouts, tormented me almost as much as the jolting cadence rocking through my body. I wanted to escape into an abyss of darkness. But every time I came close, something jostled me. Then, the whispers would start again.

The words began to change, along with the light. A

brightness crept in that made me whimper and turn my head, despite the pain.

"It's the only safe place," a voice said.

"It will likely house humans," another answered.

I wanted to tell the voices to stop. To be quiet and just let me sleep. But, opening my mouth only produced a mewling whine. Something brushed my forehead, hurting me further.

"Good. They might be able to help her."

"We don't heal the same here. We need to watch for those guns. Do not let them touch you."

"I know," yet another voice said. "You stay. We go."

"Do not kill them. Mya will not like that."

Frustration and confusion got the better of me. I opened my mouth, again, to yell. Nothing more than a groan emerged.

"Shh…my Mya. You are safe. We will find help."

After that, things grew blissfully quiet, and the light faded. I floated in the void of nothing, the pain gradually easing. In its absence, a chill crept in. Even though I couldn't see, I could imagine my breath misting in the air and ice forming on my skin. I shivered uncontrollably, each shudder punctuated by a rapid series of muffled bangs.

"We need to cool her off. She's too warm."

I wanted to cry. Why couldn't the voices just leave me alone? Or say something that made sense. Who would want to cool off when it felt ready to snow?

More pops sounded then silence returned.

"They are angry," a voice said.

Fingers grabbed me with bruising force, and I cried out.

"I don't care," another said. "They will help her. Where are they?"

"Barn. Tied to chairs."

"Take her to the house. Find a bed that is soft. I will be there in a moment. And do not touch her or try to look at her pussy. She will be angry if you do. And so will I."

The rocking started again. I groaned, hating this dream and wishing I could wake up. Instead, I pulled away from the light, the voices, and the pain and found a dark, quiet corner to hide from their persistent presence.

Resurrection Chronicles

Demon Ember

Demon Flames

Demon Ash

Demon Escape

Demon Deception

Demon Night

*More to come!

Also by M.J. Haag

Beastly Tales

Depravity

Deceit

Devastation

Tales of Cinder

Disowned (Prequel)

Defiant

Disdain

Damnation

Connect with the author

Website: MJHaag.melissahaag.com/

Newsletter: MJHaag.melissahaag.com/subscribe

ALSO BY BECCA VINCENZA

Connect with the author

Website: BeccaVincenzaAuthor.wordpress.com